Self-Liberation of Parson Sykes

Enslavement in Southampton County, Virginia

Self-Liberation of Parson Sykes
Enslavement in Southampton County, Virginia

by

COL David J. Mason, USA, Retired

HMG ePublishing, LLC
Princeton, NJ 08542

Library of Congress Catalog No. 2022914010
ISBN 978-0-9991331-1-8

Printed in the United States of America

© David J. Mason 2022

All Rights Reserved

David J. Mason, Developmental Editor
Mary M. Sumner, Contributing Editor
Gilbert Mason, Contributing Editor
Geraldine Wright, Contributing Editor
Civil War Re-enactor: Chase Neighbors

Disclaimer

This publication, *The Self-Liberation of Parson Sykes*, is a documentary novel based on a true story and actual events drawn from a variety of sources, including published materials and interviews. For dramatic and narrative purposes, the story contains fictionalized anecdotes, composite and representative characters and dialogue, and time compression. The views and opinions expressed in the novel are those of the characters only and do not reflect or represent the views and opinions held by individuals on which those characters are based.

Dedication

This work is dedicated to Privates Parson, Joseph, Henry Sykes, and other gallant and brave members of the United States Colored Troops Regiments, the precursors to Black units famously nicknamed as the Buffalo Soldiers, Smoked Yankees, the Harlem Hell Fighters, the Triple Nickles, and the Red Ball Express.

Contents

Foreword

The title, *The Self Liberation of Parson Sykes*, is a beautiful and true story of three siblings: Parson, Joseph and Henry, and their experiences in hope, a shared vision, and a daring escape. The story brings family members of all ages together as a subject of a talk at our reunions. While this has been a continuous story for over 150 years, it still resonates with Parson's descendants, as well as with siblings and other family members. As a sister, a retired educator, and lecturer from the State University of New York, I am honored to provide this foreword.

As David stated in his book, while at Sykes' family reunions, Parson's descendants discussed and recalled how Parson and his brothers escaped from enslavement and enlisted in the Union Army. In particular, I first learned of his desire to author this book while at a family gathering on our brother Gilbert's farm in Chesapeake, Virginia, after he gave his usual three-minute presentation. The history of Parson's escape itself is a continuing conversation between our many generations and a favorite story. Because of David's confirmed interest in military history, his research on the role of Black soldiers in the Civil War, along with his fascination with our family ancestry, I encouraged him to do this work to memorialize and chronicle Parson's daring ordeal. The way David arranged this true and traditional family story amazed me. A trilogy, his story profiles Private Parson Sykes' evolution from enslavement in Southampton County, Virginia, followed by his enlistment into the Union Army, and culminating with his emancipation and return to the county.

This book, the first of the trilogy, profiles Parson Sykes' evolution from a curiously enslaved teenager in Southampton County, Virginia, self-liberation, followed by his enlistment into the Union Army upon his legitimate emancipation. The *Self-*of the American Civil War on the slave-holding Jacob Williams' middle-class family farm. In the book, Parson and Jacob Williams are at opposite ends of the disputed points over the moral issue of slavery and secession, a political decision that led directly to war. Early in 1861, before the Civil War started, Parson began discussing human rights and political implications of the abolition of slavery with his two brothers and a confidante, Henry Charity. In December 1864, he planned to liberate himself by running away from Jacob Williams' farm and following an eastward path along the Seaboard & Roanoke Railroad to reach Norfolk, Virginia, a Union occupied city. Parson knew President Abraham Lincoln had issued the Emancipation Proclamation, which declared as freed, effective January 1, 1863, enslaved people only in areas in rebellion against the United States. It also provided for the enlistment of African Americans. Upon reaching Norfolk and captured in the hands of Union troops, it declared Parson and his brothers freed from bondage.

The *Self-Liberation of Parson Sykes* should function also to draw much needed attention to the key role all Black soldiers played during the Civil War as members of United States Colored Troops (USCT). In May 1863, the United States established the Bureau of Colored Troops to manage the burgeoning numbers of Black soldiers who laid the path from contraband status to gallant and feared warriors during the Civil War. The *Self-Liberation of Parson Sykes* details how the Union Army XXV Corps came into existence. The XXV Corps was composed entirely of the USCT regiments and were the first Union forces to enter and capture Richmond, Virginia. Though less heralded, the USCT regiments were the precursors to Black units famously nicknamed as the Buffalo Soldiers, Smoked Yankees, the Harlem Hell Fighters, and the Red Ball Express.

History itself is a continuing dialogue between the present and the past and so is this book which is a longtime dream and hope of David's, and the way David recounts our family anecdotes in The *Self-Liberation of Parson Sykes* is riveting from start to finish. As I expected from him, he entwined the bigger picture of the political and cultural issues of the nation while providing fascinating details about our great-grandfather's life and allowed the reader to feel connected to the story and to understand the incredibly huge risks he took in his liberation. David writes with authenticity, diligence, and cares about subjects that are sensitive to many people, presenting the facts as they are. The family will feel connected closer to Parson Sykes as they read the book and will be fascinated to learn the historical details that our great-grandfather bravely undertook.

Again, I am honored to write this foreword and hope that each family member and every other reader appreciate this outstanding story of the determination, strength, and faith of our family in this documentary novel as it chronicles Parson's escape from enslavement in Southampton County, Virginia.

Yours Truly,

Mary M. Sumner
Instructor and Lecturer, Retired, SUNY
Uniondale, New York
September 30, 2022

Until justice is blind to color, until education is unaware of race,
until opportunity is unconcerned with the color of men's skins,
emancipation will be a proclamation but not a fact.

— Lyndon B. Johnson

Preface

Over 150 years ago, Parson Sykes, and his brothers Joseph, and Henry made a daring escape from bondage in Confederate occupied Southampton County, Virginia during the American Civil War. At Sykes' family reunions, Parson's descendants discussed and recalled how they escaped from enslavement and enlisted in the Union Army. His self-liberation quest was the beginning of Parson's lifelong struggle to secure human rights and equality in America. The *Self-Liberation of Parson Sykes* is a documentary novel that chronicles Parson's enslavement in Southampton County, enlistment in the Union Army XXV Corps, and return to the county as a local hero and leader. I became motivated to prepare for this work after finding published United States government records that supported the family's oral chronicles. Some of the recorded information was similar to the oral history of how my great-grandfather Parson Sykes and his brothers, Joseph and Henry, liberated themselves.

The *Self-Liberation of Parson Sykes* took place near the end of the American Civil War on the slave-holding Jacob Williams' middle-class family farm. The Confederate government still bound Black people to chattel slavery, existing without rights, solely to serve the political, economic, and social benefits of the slaveholders. Early in 1861, before the Civil War started, Parson began discussing human rights and political implications of the abolition of slavery with his two brothers and a confidante, Henry Charity. In December 1864, he launched a plan to liberate himself by running away from Jacob Williams' farm and following an eastward path along the Seaboard & Roanoke Railroad to reach Norfolk, Virginia, a Union occupied city. Parson knew President Abraham Lincoln had issued the Emancipation Proclamation, that declared, effective January 1, 1863, as freed enslaved people only in areas in rebellion against the United States and provided for the enlistment of Black men.

The *Self-Liberation of Parson Sykes* also functions to draw attention to the key role all Black soldiers played during the Civil War as members of United States Colored Troops (USCT). In May 1863, the United States established the Bureau of Colored Troops to manage the burgeoning numbers of Black soldiers who laid the path from contraband status to gallant and feared warriors during the Civil War. The *Self-Liberation of Parson Sykes* details how the Union Army XXV Corps came into existence. The XXV Corps was composed entirely of the USCT regiments and were the first Union forces to enter and capture Richmond, Virginia. Though less heralded, the USCT regiments were the precursors to Black units famously nicknamed as the Buffalo Soldiers, Smoked Yankees, the Harlem Hell Fighters, and the Red Ball Express.

Although slavery was the law of the land and status quo for over two hundred years, its victims, who found it morally unacceptable, challenged and resisted it every day. The *Self-Liberation of Parson Sykes* chronicles Parson Sykes' evolution from a curiously enslaved teenager, self-liberation, followed by his enlistment into the Union Army with emancipation, and culminating with his return to Southampton County, Virginia. Since the colonization of Virginia in 1619, slavery stayed a steadfast enigma that blurred and paralyzed the moral, economic, political decision-making processes causing crisis after crisis throughout the nation. As a moral issue, slavery denied human rights based on the diversity of races and religions. The political context of the times since the colonization of Virginia shaped slavery in Southampton County. The state and county relied on slavery heavily for economic prosperity and used wealth to justify enslavement practices.

Parson's emerging understanding of human rights helped him to envision a new future and life after emancipation. He found discarded railroad maps, abolition pamphlets, and sectional periodicals helpful in planning his liberation quest. In his secret haven, he risked life and limb to guard and protect his collection of documents about freedom, abolitionists, resistance, and humanity. Parson grasped the injustice of his enslavement and felt called to react against slavery for no other reason than to gain his freedom. He learned enslaved African descendants had always desired freedom and self-liberation was his best method to gain it. The cruel treatment he received from Jacob varied, but the laws in Virginia left enslaved people without defense or recourse.

At sundown on December 3, 1864, Parson and his brothers started on the self-liberation quest. They seized some provisions, carpentry tools, network maps and other equipment and quickly changed clothes, assumed alias names, and started their trip east toward Norfolk. They knew the direction of travel by keeping the railroad tracks and telegraph lines in view. However, Parson did not know exactly where the railroad tracks and telegraph lines led. Escaping involved traveling under harsh conditions and navigating into unknown territory, while eluding slave catchers made the journey perilous.

Parson committed to pursue self-liberation and entered the Union Army to fight for freedom. He skillfully planned his self-liberation ordeal to reach Fort Monroe alive and fit for military service. He and his two brothers solidified their commitment to the call for self-liberation and to enter the fight for human rights. Their ultimate aims were to achieve willful freedom, to gain desired ends via self-determination, and to create ways and means for enhancing the rock bottom economic conditions enslavement imparted upon them.

Through Parson's self-liberation ordeal, using vignettes of USCT regiments roles in different battles, the novel details how the Union Army XXV Corps came into existence. The XXV Corps was composed entirely of the USCT regiments that were the first Union forces to enter and capture Richmond, Virginia. Hopefully, the book will draw more attention to the significant role Black soldiers and their White officers played in winning the Civil War as members of USCT regiments.

Acknowledgments

Over the three years it took me to complete this trilogy, family members gave me help and encouragement in writing the *Self-Liberation of Parson Sykes*. Foremost, I am indebted to my incredible wife, Paige Hinton-Mason. I really want to thank Paige for her steadfast patience, lively discussions, and loving encouragement. Her confidence in me has been the foundation on which my efforts to complete this book arose. Her tolerance, support, editing and suggestions for improving the manuscript helped inspire literary practices that I never knew I needed. It is because of her input that I have a written story to pass on to my family and friends where one did not exist.

I am eternally grateful to my brother and sisters. Among them is my sister Mary M. Sumner, who rose to the level of contributing editor for this project. She deserves much appreciation for her suggestions for improving the manuscript and for shepherding it through multiple drafts until we found it fit for publishing. Her encouragement and literary skills of editing grammar and content to ensure quality made this book possible. Thank you so much for your continual help in this book and I look forward to collaborating with you on the next two novels in the trilogy.

And to my brother, Gilbert, who often served more like a contributing editor to me than a mentor. As contributing editor, he exchanged storyline ideas, advised on content for the book, collected and forwarded historical articles, took photographs of the Sykes farm and other extinguishing landmarks. In particular, he provided the photo of the cotton field shown on the cover of the book. Besides this, I owe thanks to him for the trips he made to government facilities to research and collect historical information and records that supported the family's oral chronicles that helped to make this project possible. He used a variety of helpful research tools, such as publicly available archives, visiting libraries and depositories for records. Thank you so much for your help to sprout our ancestral roots.

I am especially grateful to my oldest sister, Geraldine Wright, for her exemplary recollection of anecdotes presented at family reunions and gatherings. Her editorial contribution included her collection of letters written by Parson and his descendants were valuable resources for developing content for the trilogy. She provided a firsthand description of life in Southampton County and shared memories of family history, celebratory events, and traditions. Thanks so much Gerry for your support, for taking time as a beta reader, and for your feedback.

I am grateful to my grandson, Chase Neighbors, for offering his likeness of Private Parson Sykes on the cover of the book in a blue civil war uniform. Using his image was important to recreate the appearance of Parson at the time the Union Army XXV Corps came into existence. Thank you for the reenactment image and visage of the book.

In writing *The Self-Liberation of Parson Sykes*, other family members gave me help and encouragement. I am indebted to them as well for endorsing and supporting my work. Among these are aunts and uncles, nieces and nephews, cousins, and in-laws. A special thanks to my Aunt Marie Sykes for her extensive phone conversations about Southampton County and our family history.

In addition, thanks to her and Uncle Lloyd Sykes for hosting and contributing to our ongoing tradition of family reunions.

There are several fellow authors, friends, and other people I owe thanks to who shared the gift of their time to read and comment on the manuscript, the synopsis, or otherwise, to help me complete this book. Among those was Sidney Jackson, author of several published novels including *Darkness Is not Eternal*, and *The Liar's Gift*, to name a few. He objectively proofread my manuscript and provided me with helpful feedback on spotted errors and offered his suggestions.

Finally, among the many debts I owe in developing this book is to Daniel W. Crofts. In his book, *Old Southampton: Politics and Society in a Virginia County, 1834-1869*, he included evidence of the military service of three enslaved brothers, Harrison, Joseph, and Henry Williams. This passage in Crofts' book appeared similar to our oral family history of how Parson Sykes escaped from the enslavement that I knew. It induced me to research the brothers in the passage. Subsequently, I discovered that Harrison Williams was an alias that my great-grandfather Parson Sykes assumed after he fled Southampton, County. The diligent research reflected in Crofts' works has made mine possible.

Because no matter who we are or where we come from, we're all entitled to the basic human rights of clean air to breathe, clean water to drink, and healthy land to call home.

— Martin Luther King III

Introduction

The *Self-Liberation of Parson Sykes* is a trilogy that profiles Private Parson Sykes' evolution from enslavement in Southampton County, Virginia, followed by his enlistment into the Union Army, and culminating with his emancipation and return to the county. The first novel, subtitled *Enslavement in Southampton County, Virginia,* is based on the true story of Parson Sykes' self-liberation and actual events drawn from a variety of sources, including military records and family chronicles. At Sykes' family reunions, Parson's descendants customarily discuss and recall in various renditions of how he escaped from enslavement and enlisted in the Union Army.

This novel, the first of the trilogy, profiles Private Parson Sykes' evolution from enslavement in nine chapters. The chapters of the book proceed in a linear and chronological way.

The Cross Keys, Southampton County 1864.

Liberation of Parson Sykes took place in 1864 near the end of the American Civil War on the slave-holding Jacob Williams' middle-class family farm in the Cross Keys area of Southampton County, Virginia. When Parson was not working in the peanut, cotton or tobacco fields, Jacob hired him out to the railroad company to perform basic carpentry, light building maintenance, and janitorial work. Parson and Jacob Williams were at opposite ends of the disputed points over the moral issue of slavery and secession, a political decision that led directly to war.

Resistance and Abolition.

During the Civil War, Jacob, fearing that Parson and the other slaves might escape, intensified the plantation discipline and his grip on the farm. Parson believed no one should live in slavery or servitude and that slavery should be abolished in all forms and places. He learned the abolitionists were resisting and furthering the abolition battle place into the political sphere. Parson and his brothers devised forms of passive resistance, such as damaging equipment, working slowly, and keeping their human rights and religious beliefs alive.

Commitment to Self-Liberation.

In the conflict's waning days, Parson enhanced his knowledge and appreciation of emancipation, agricultural commerce, information technology, and warfare through observation of his surroundings. Parson eventually learned that slavery was a commercial venture that existed where it was economically viable for those in power. Jacob Williams found slavery profitable and enjoyed the rate of return on slaves comparable to his other assets. A man of unbending independence, Parson sternly committed himself to self-liberation and emancipation.

Reactions to and Reflections on Freedom.

As Parson reflected on his life, he recognized and believed that Black citizens in Cross Keys had a natural urge to be free and fight to determine their own livelihood. By observation and comparison of his surroundings, Parson grasped the injustice of his enslavement and felt called to react against slavery for no other reason than to gain his freedom. Parson met Frances Hill and recognized a need to bring to the consciousness of enslaved men and women the unhealthy messages they received through slavery and the effect of their relationships. He learned enslaved African descendants had always desired freedom and self-liberation was the best method to gain it.

Broadsides, Brochures, and Newspapers.

During the war, broadsides, brochures, and newspapers were vital sources of information on the conflict, and as venues in which to attack and defend the issues that caused the Civil War. Working at the Boykins Depot gave Parson the opportunity to search through the depot waste containers for discarded, printed messages with actionable information about the cities and whistle stops along the Seaboard & Roanoke Railroad network. He searched for non-military, political, economic, and social news reports, and articles about the abolition of slavery, and advertisements of successful slave escapes. Parson now knew his self-liberation plan's mission - To reach Fort Monroe alive and fit for military service.

In the Pursuit of Liberation and Equality.

Although laws denied him freedom, Parson used a wide variety of strategies to contest Jacob's authority and to assert his rights to control his own destiny. Jacob depended on his involuntary labor to keep the family business solvent. Parson, Joseph, and Henry often used work slowdowns and malingering cleverly to gain some terms and conditions for their labor. Like many enslaved Black people in the county, Parson opted to flee enslavement and pursue liberty and equality, although escape attempts were dangerous and uncertain. After studying the railroad map, Parson presumed that following along the connections en route from Boykins to Norfolk County was a plausible escape route to reach Fort Monroe.

Parson Reveals Escape Plan.

Parson worked ferociously on his escape plan, collecting, and storing provisions in his haven, gathering small tools for weapons, securing his railroad line connections map, and other apparatus to employ during his journey. He developed a plan to minimize the effects of contact, connection, or communication with the civilian populace. In the escape plan that Parson conceived, he assumed the home guard as Jacob's first line of defense against his self-liberation. Parson planned the escape based on the assumption of early ground contact with slave catchers or patrollers, either en route or shortly after arrival at the destination. He knew about the difficulties of surviving exposure to winter weather, hiding in swamps or wooded thickets, and navigating into unknown territory based on folklore methodologies.

Quest for Freedom Behind Union Lines.

According to information included in the National Archives and Civil War pension applications for the First Cavalry Regiment, United States Colored Troops (USCT), Parson and his two brothers liberated themselves from a Southampton County, Virginia plantation and joined the Union Army at the same time and place. Parson's journey to cross Union lines incurred enormous risks and was a tremendous gamble. He did not know the exact location of the Union army, and nearly fell into the hands of Confederate guerrillas or vigilantes. The consequences of either were grave. Parson and his brothers successfully entered Union controlled territory, exhausted and ravenous.

Behold, Comrades-in-Arms.

Parson and his brothers safely arrived at Camp Bowers Hill in Norfolk County. Bower's Hill was in Virginia, on the Seaboard & Roanoke Railroad line, at a point about equidistance between Portsmouth, opposite Norfolk, and Suffolk. Eager Union recruiters greeted them as they entered the camp. Parson and his brothers enrolled into the Company I, First Cavalry Regiment, USCT. During enrollment, Parson always showed his desire for freedom and welcomed the pickets and guards from the Provost Marshal's office as liberators.

Using vignettes of USCT regiments roles in different battles, the novel also details how the Union Army XXV Corps came into existence. The War Department organized the XXV Corps entirely of the USCT regiments that were the first Union forces to enter and capture Richmond, Virginia.

Prologue

According to family history, my great-grandfather, Parson Sykes, and his brothers Joseph and Henry, made a brave and challenging escape from bondage on Jacob Williams' farm during the American Civil War. The *Self-Liberation of Parson Sykes* is a documentary novel based on their trek to freedom and actual events drawn from a variety of sources, including published materials and family chronicles. The story occurred in 1864, near the end of the American Civil War on the slave-holding Jacob Williams' middle-class family farm in Southampton County, Virginia. It is a narrative, a profile of Private Parson Sykes' evolution from a curiously enslaved teenager in Southampton County, Virginia, followed by his enlistment into the Union Army. Parson and Jacob Williams were at opposite ends of the disputed points over the moral issue of slavery and secession, a political decision that led directly to war.

From my research of Civil War pension records, I uncovered that "Harrison Williams" was the alias Parson assumed after he escaped from enslavement. I also learned the brothers reached Fort Monroe in early December 1864 and, after enlistment, they performed successful combat military duty with the XXV Corps of the Army Union. They served their entire enlistment together with Company I, First

Cavalry Regiment, United States Colored Troops (USCT) from December 1864 to February 1866. I was glad to learn the legacy of my ancestors as they made up their minds to seek freedom.

About thirty years before this story began, another event took place that set up another unquenchable legacy. In 1831, Southampton County was the location of the most serious slave rebellion in the United States' history. On August 21-22, the memorable Southampton Insurrection, led by the slave Nat Turner, occurred with the deaths of fifty-eight whites and an unknown number of blacks. Armed with hatchets and knives, slave and educated minister Nat Turner and seven of his followers launched the insurrection. A local militia captured the insurgents, and they eventually had trials and hanged them.

Before the Southampton Insurrection, white families in Southampton County worried little about a slave rebellion. Jacob Williams' farm was in a neighborhood of Southampton, known as Cross Key, where Parson Sykes was born and enslaved. The original family homesteader, William Williams Sr., owned 328 acres at this location in 1782. Jacob, the middle son, farmed his father's land and shared the house with his mother until she died in 1827. By 1831, Jacob Williams had increased his landholding to 613 acres through inheritance and a series of land deals. On August 22, Jacob Williams' farm came under attack by Nat Turner and his insurgents.

In Parson's mind, the insurrection made its mark, striking at the enslavement system with willful retaliation as punishment for past hostile actions and for deterrence of future hostile. Nat Turner, in his mind, was a symbol of all that was wrong with the enslavement system and of the potential for black retaliation and self-liberation. In the mind of Jacob Williams, Nat Turner embodied the dark savagery of Black people in Southampton County, and Jacob often repressed fears that their savagery would lead to his property loss and destruction.

The Southampton Insurrection was Jacob Williams' dreaded fear, an uprising by enslaved people and massacre of white men, women, and children. The fear struck the hearts of slave owners across the country, leading to harsher enslavement codes and squelching plans for gradual emancipation. As news of Turner, his rebellion, and fate spread, the abolitionist movement intensified. To satisfy my urgency out of curiosity, I memorialized my findings about the self-liberation of Parson Sykes, Williams' farm attack by Nat Turner, and the controversial military service of Black soldiers with this story.

Prophet Nat Turner (1800–1831)

Few historical events spark so many differences of opinion, as does Virginia's 1831 Southampton Insurrection. Nat Turner (1800–1831) was known to his local fellow slaves in Southampton County as "The Prophet." On the evening of Sunday, August 21, 1831, he met six associates in the woods at Cabin Pond, and about 2:00 a.m., they entered local houses and killed the white inhabitants.

Nat Turner, a slave and circuit preacher, believed that signs from Heaven guided him to start the largest and bloodiest revolt by enslaved people in American history. Some refer to Turner as a rebel and a murderer, while others view him as a revolutionary hero in the fight against slavery. Despite these various points of view, historians depicted him in American history in a straight-forward manner when they discussed enslavement revolts, bondage, and abolition. While he lived in a religious world, he was not a professional preacher.

Born on October 2, 1800, Nat Turner originally belonged to Benjamin Turner. He was intelligent and had marks on his head and breast, which the Black people who knew him interpreted as marking him for some high calling. As recorded of him, he experimented with paper, gunpowder, and pottery. He was never known to swear an oath, to drink a drop of spirits, or to commit a theft. Instead, he cultivated fasting and prayer and the reading of the Bible.

On May 12, 1828, he was no longer in doubt. A great voice said unto him that the Serpent was loose, that Christ had laid down the yoke, that he, Nat, was to take it up again, and that the time was fast approaching when the first should be last and the last should be first. He interpreted a solar eclipse in February 1831 as the sign for him to go forward. However, he waited until he had made sure of his most important associates. It is worthy of note that when Nat began his work, while he wanted the killing to be effective and widespread, he commanded that no outrage be committed, and that his associates obeyed him.

About noon on Sunday, August 21, 1831, four of Nat's associates, Henry Porter, Hark Travis, Nelson Williams, and Sam Francis gathered, on the plantation of Joseph Travis at Cross Keys, preparing for a barbecue. Soon, by and by Will Francis and another associate of the name Jack Reese joined them. Two hours later, Nat Turner came and, seeing Will and his associates, raised a question as to their being there, to which Will replied that life was worth no more to him than the others and that liberty was as dear to him. This answer satisfied Nat, and he went into a conference with his most trusted friends.

Nat Turner's Assault on Jacob Williams' Farm

Up to Sunday, August 21, 1831, there was nothing to distinguish Cross Keys from any other rural, scenic southeastern Virginia countryside neighborhood. On that day, Nat Turner rebelled against his white oppressors and enslavers. As described in William Sidney Drewry's account of the Southampton Insurrection, this section of the county embraced in the raid was the most recently settled, and the inhabitants had not reached that stage of larger cultivated estates and imposing dwellings enjoyed by the farmers of the more eastern counties. In the thinly settled county, Black people, concealed by the enormous expanse of forest which surrounded them, could quietly enjoy their reveling undetected.

About eleven o'clock on August 22, 1831, Jacob Williams found Nelson, one of his slaves, and one of the principal insurgents dressed in his best clothes. Being in a hurry to go to the woods to measure timber for Drewry Simmons, Jacob did not stop to investigate the overbearing manner of Nelson. Before this, Nelson warned Caswell Worrell, Jacob's nephew, and the overseer, that the white people might look out and take care of themselves. He foretold something would happen before long, which anyone in his practice could tell. Nelson had been waiting for Nat Turner and his insurgents.

He went to the field where Caswell Worrell was overseeing the field hands and got permission to go to the house, saying he was sick. He also persuaded the overseer to go with him, thinking of delivering him into the hands of the insurgents, but Caswell escaped into the woods. Nelson was not very sick, however, when he saw the insurgents approaching. He was the leader in this section and seemed to have worked faithfully for the cause.

Shortly before noon on August 22, Nat Turner's insurgents reached the farm of William Williams. The band of insurgents had their number swelled by forced recruits and by volunteers, so much so that Nat gave the usual order to mount and march at once. William Williams had been recently married and lived in a neat and comfortable little cottage near the road. He was in the fodder-field while his wife was at the house alone. The insurgents appeared, asked her where her husband was, and then gave her the choice of dying there or with him. She preferred the latter, but as they went in search of him, she fled and was some distance from them when the insurgents pursued, overtaken, and killed her.

Next, the other team of insurgents went to Jacob Williams' house and killed his wife and three children. Jacob was away from home early Monday morning, and when he returned, about eleven o'clock, he found Nelson, one of his slaves, dressed in his best clothes. Being in a hurry to go to the woods to measure timber for Drewry Simmons, Jacob did not stop to investigate the overbearing manner of Nelson. A few days before this encounter, Nelson forewarned Caswell Worrell, Jacob's overseer, that the white people might look out and take care of themselves, as something was going to happen before long which anyone of his practice could tell.

Nelson professed to have prophetic power, but such remarks had been so common with him that no one paid attention to him until the insurgents arrived, about twelve o'clock on August 22. Nelson had been waiting for them. He went to the field where Caswell Worrell was supervising the field hands and got permission to go to the house, saying he was sick. He also persuaded Caswell to go with him, thinking of delivering him into the hands of the insurgents, but he escaped and ran into the woods. Though Jacob allowed Nelson the greatest freedom, liberty, and communication with them, he could not persuade Jacob's other slaves to revolt.

When the insurgents arrived at Jacob's farm, they killed Edwin Drewry, who was the overseer for James Bell, and had come for a load of corn. He ran, but the insurgents pursued and shot him. After visiting Caswell's house and killing his wife and two children, the insurgents went back to Jacob's home. He barely had time to view the bodies of his murdered family when he fled to the cornfield, from which he could view the actions of the insurgents.

By noon on Tuesday, August 23, the local militia had killed, captured, or dispersed the insurgents. Nat Turner escaped and hid until October 30, when Benjamin Phipps caught him in the immediate vicinity, having used several hiding places over the earlier nine and a half weeks. The next day, a squad of men delivered him to the county sheriff and lodged in the county jail in Jerusalem, Virginia. There, from November 1 through November 3, Thomas Ruffin Gray, a 31-year-old lawyer who had previously represented several other defendants charged in the uprising, interviewed him.

The Nat Turner Confessions and Trial

While in prison, Nat Turner made a full and voluntary confession to Thomas R. Gray. In the confession, he said the Holy Spirit spoke to him, of seeing visions and signs in the heavens, and that the Holy Spirit ordained him for some noble purpose in the hands of the Almighty. Also, the confession recounted the whole insurrection, with lists of the whites killed during the insurrection, and of the Black people brought before the court of Southampton and sentenced.

On November 5,1831, Judge Jeremiah Cobb tried Nat Turner before the court of Southampton, condemned him to execution and hanged him on November 9th. An enormous crowd was on hand for Nat's trial. The clerk of court read the charges: Nat alias Nat Turner, a Black man slave, the property of Putnam Moore the infant, charged with conspiring to rebel and make insurrection. It was an open and shut case. His attorney, James Parker, submitted the case without argument.

Judge Cobb asked Nat if he wished to make a statement before sentencing. Nat replied he had nothing but what he said before. Judge Cobb ordered the state of Virginia to pay the Putnam Moore estate $375 reparation, Nat's value as a slave.

The Aftermath of the Nat Turner Insurrection

Of fifty-three Black people summoned in connection with the insurrection, Southampton executed seventeen and twelve, transported out of the state. Despite this, vigilantes slaughtered Black people without trial and sometimes under circumstances of the greatest barbarity. A party from Richmond, intending to kill every Black person in Southampton County, tortured, burned, or maimed the Black people at will. In Nat's time, the patrols would tie up the free people of color, flog them, and try to make them lie against one another, and often killed them before anybody could interfere.

In revenge, whites killed scores of Black people who had no part in the rebellion. They overpowered Black people, and those not shot on sight, jailed for a tried and hanged in due course. The paranoia that resulted from the insurrection encouraged the widespread persecution of slaves and freed Black citizens and eventually resulted in the death of two hundred Black Americans by the hands of erratic white mobs. This is interesting, since only around seventy Black people took part in the revolt. As a result, nearly one-hundred innocent people died because of the widespread panic and fear that gripped the nation following the insurrection.

Following the Southampton Insurrection, suspicion and intense paranoia swept throughout much of the southern United States. Turner's goal in leading his insurrection was to instill fear across the southern states and to encourage his fellow slaves to revolt against their masters. While Turner did not create a widespread rebellion, he did, however, incorporate a heightened sense of alert that existed in the minds of white people for years to come.

The Prelude to a Lingering Sense of Tension and Fear

Nothing that happened on August 22, 1831, disposed Jacob to give up his enslavement holding. In fact, his holding grew significantly after the uprising. Between 1830 and 1850, it doubled in size and then remained stable through 1860, to Jacob's eightieth year. For decades after the insurrection, he feared the arming of Black people.

Because slavery supplied substantial revenue for farmers and plantation owners in the South, however, not even the threat of violence could stop the thriving enslavement institution in place. With two opposing viewpoints developing, therefore, a general sense of tension developed between the states in the North and the South. Over the next few decades, tension continued to grow.

The more aggressively the northern abolitionists pressed their anti-slavery agenda, the more defensive the pro-slavery south became. Thus, Turner's rebellion served as a spark that brought about the tensions that eventually culminated into the Civil War. Had it not been for the rebellion, the Civil War may not have developed as quickly as it did, further extending the slaves' detrimental condition.

In the book, Parson and Jacob Williams faced each other at opposite ends of the disputed points over the moral issue of slavery and secession, a political decision that led directly to war. Now that we have recounted Nat Turner's raid on Jacob Williams' farm and the lingering sense of tension and fear, let us consider how it influenced Jacob, Parson, and the people who lived long after it occurred.

Chapter One
Cross Keys, Southampton County

In early fall 1864, the air was cool in Cross Keys, yet the foliage seemed green. Glimpses of Muscadine and Scuppernong vines loaded with ripened grapes appeared along the dusty dirt road. Great clusters of persimmon trees hung over the road, with bright orange fruit ready to drop from the branches. There in the low and wooded fields, like any scenic Mid-Atlantic countryside, was the Cross Keys, a scarcely populated neighborhood in Southampton County, Virginia. The neighborhood is at the north-east junction of Meherrin Road and Cross Keys Road north of Boykins Depot in Southampton County. It lies near the North Carolina state line seventy miles from Norfolk, and just as far from Richmond. Cross Keys is about fifteen miles from Murfreesboro in North Carolina, and about twenty-five from the Great Dismal Swamp. At a secure distance off the road, obscured amid the woods, stood an old decaying grand house. Aligned behind it is a neat Confederate encampment of white tents, drilling for deployment near Petersburg, Virginia.

Slaveholders in Cross Keys and across Southampton County expected that an uprising by enslaved people would go with the start of the war and strengthened plantation discipline earlier, during the spring and summer of 1861. As an increasing number of white men left home for the Confederate army, however, and the dreaded rebellion never materialized, white Virginians loosened their grip on their slaves. In the county, enslaved people patrols dwindled in number. In the absence of male authority figures, plantation discipline relaxed as enslaved people sensed and exploited their mistresses' weakness. While a few slaves stopped working entirely, others refused to grow cash crops without extra incentives.

In the earliest stages of the Civil War, the practice of living off the land was a way of supplementing the army rations shortage. Food was the first area in which soldiers engaged in large-scale theft from civilians. Initially, soldiers in both armies freely picked apples, pears, and other fruit from trees they passed while on patrol in the county. Many soldiers in the encampment came from farms themselves and knew the labor and investment that went into raising field crops and filling storage facilities. The thought of foraging the productions bothered them. But as the war dragged out, the attitudes of Confederate soldiers toward supplementing their diet with the practice of living off the land changed markedly. Once a few members of the encampment crossed an inhumane line by taking food from civilians for their own consumption, the behavior inevitably spread to other soldiers. The Cross Keys' residents competed with the encamped Confederate soldiers for the food and rummage.

In the spring of 1861, the bitter north and south sectional conflict that had been intensifying over four decades erupted into a Civil War, when states began seceding and forming the Confederate States of America. At its outset, the Civil War was not a war to end slavery, rather, to save the Union. In the states that seceded from the Union, three million Black people were in bondage, existing without human rights solely to serve the political, economic, and social benefits of the slaveholders. As the war progressed and conditions worsened, Southampton citizens faced greater and greater hardships and devastation. The enslaved people in the county endured much harsher conditions under strict enslavement codes and oppressive racism in the Cross Keys.

During the 1860 presidential election, Abraham Lincoln's antislavery views were well established. His victory as the nation's first Republican president was the catalyst that pushed the first southern states to secede. Lincoln sought foremost to preserve the Union, and he knew few people would have supported a war against slavery in 1861. Young Parson Sykes, however, hoped that the war's outcome would rid the status quo by abolishing chattel slavery.

Parson Sykes - Early Childhood

For over 150 years, Parson Sykes' descendants passed down stories and adventures of his early life at family reunions and holiday meals, weddings, and other gatherings where the ancestors met. As told by his son, John P. Sykes, Parson was born and raised on Jacob Williams' farm in the Cross Keys neighborhood about fifteen years after Nat Turner raided it during the insurrection. He was the son of Solomon Sykes and Louisa Williams. Louisa and her three sons, Parson, Joseph, and Henry were slaves on Jacob Williams' farm. However, not much was known about Solomon, who may have been a slave on a nearby farm and hired out to Jacob.

Solomon Sykes was a skillful farmer who Jacob Williams hired to supervise his tobacco, peanuts, and cotton interests on his three farms. Louisa did all the cooking, cleaning, washing of clothes, sweeping, food service, and childcare. She also had to be alert at any hour of the day or night. She lived in a small two-story slave shanty with an open second floor, where Parson and his brothers slept.

According to oral family history, early in his life, Parson worked on the farms. He followed along beside Solomon and the other older workers, and as he grew older, became an experienced substitute for Jacob Williams' aging slaves. During the war, he learned to tend the horses, drove the carriages, and kept the gardens. On Jacob farms, enslaved children, from the age of about ten, suffered exposure to the ills of slavery, working full-time work, with the threat of family separation, and denial of basic human and civil rights.

For his own predatory benefits and needs, Jacob trained Parson, Joseph, and Henry to be carpenters and farm laborers. He was one of many farmers in the county who violated the law and instructed the enslaved people on his farm to read. In addition, Jacob ensured they learned and obeyed his rules and laws that denied slaves human and civil rights. Parson understood as a slave, he could own nothing, not even his labor, that served the political, economic, and the social benefits of Jacob, his enslaver. Parson was good with artisan tools. He was not afraid of heights or climbing on the roofs of tall barns and farm buildings. On and off the Williams Farm, there was always a need for enslaved journeymen who could do a wide variety of farming, blacksmith, and carpentry duties.

Jacob supplied the family with a poor diet. Louisa supplemented it by subsistence farming a small plot of land and her sons' small game hunting. He did not supply ample clothing, and Louisa worked at night after long days of labor to clothe the family. For Parson, Joseph, and Henry, the war bought an even heavier workload. Sometimes, Jacob allotted them the bare minimum of food and clothing; anything beyond that was up to the family to gain.

Parson and other children in the county shared an excitement about the war and an interest in the political and military affairs going on during the war. They enjoyed watching soldiers' drills and ran along beside military units as they paraded through the streets and fields. Watching the steamboats sail along the Blackwater River during the Civil War was an unforgettable event for the children. Both Union and Confederate forces in Virginia used steamboats to move troops and cargo to their operational supply centers and strategic hubs.

Parson Knowingly Violated Enslavement Codes

As the war progressed and conditions worsened, the Confederacy faced greater and greater hardships and devastation. Parson hoped the war's outcome would overthrow the status quo by outlawing the centuries-old chattel slavery institution.

In 1864, Parson was reaching draft age, and Jacob Williams needed his labor on his family farm in the peanuts, cotton, or tobacco fields. When he was not working in the fields, he built and maintained structures on the plantation house and complex, or Jacob hired him out to the railroad company to do basic carpentry, light building maintenance, and janitorial work. Because Parson was reaching draft age, Louisa feared the Confederacy would impress him into the army if he did not liberate himself. She was happy to see that all her sons were interested in the Union Army.

According to a family anecdote, Jacob hired out Parson to the Seaboard & Roanoke railroad company to replace white male shopmen pressed for military service. Parson performed janitorial and light carpentry tasks in the depot. Its waiting room had restrooms for male and female patrons. The south side of the building had a baggage and mail handling area. These areas often held forbidden documents and mail confiscated from passengers by confederate patrollers. Above the baggage handling area was the telegraph office, the confederate mail room, and an area used for record storage. Parson cleaned these areas and emptied trash bins of discarded newspapers and records. He refrained from reading in front of others in the depot. He earned a dollar and a half per week when hired out by Jacob Williams, who took half of the pay. The depot also served as the assembly hall for the Home Guard in the area and was used for moving Confederate troops and supplies.

Parson secretly collected discarded newspapers, magazines, and other documents to perform research on ways to strike out for freedom. Each day when his work at the depot ended, Parson spent time in a secret haven, alleged to be the old forgotten home owned by Nathaniel Francis, another casualty of the insurrection. There, near a barely recognized pig-path, hidden beneath the vines and fallen trees, to avoid Jacob's suspicion, he had about one hour in which he researched and read the discarded documents he hid there. Continuous research and acts of resistance fulfilled Parson's daily life on the Williams' farm. Although the laws denied him freedom, Parson used a wide variety of tricks to contest Jacob's power, and to assert his human rights to control his own life. Jacob Williams depended on involuntary labor to keep his farm solvent. Parson and other enslaved workers often used work slowdowns to resist theft of their labor.

When the sowing season started, Parson spent time with his two brothers and close friend, Henry Charity, discussing human rights and political implications of the abolition of slavery. About the same age as Parson, Henry Charity, was a freed Black man who worked on different farms in the county. He told Parson and his brothers how memories of the Nat Turner haunted Jacob Williams. Like other enslavers, he expected that a slave uprising would come with the start of the war and increased plantation discipline.

Parson often described to Henry Charity how Southampton enslavement codes made it illegal to teach slaves to read. The codes restricted the marriage rights of enslaved people, to prevent them from trying to change their masters by marrying into a family on another farm. They restricted marriage between people of different races. The Virginia enslavement codes prohibited large groups of enslaved people from gathering away from their farms. He told Henry Charity that the enslavement codes on slaves' punishment had no penalty for accidentally killing a slave while punishing them.

Parson had no way to protest to Jacob's harsh treatment and abuse legally. In Virginia, most enslavement codes concerned the rights and duties of slaveholders and not about aiding enslaved people. The codes left a great deal unsaid, with much of the actual practice of slavery being a matter of traditions rather than formal law. There were similarities between the state and county enslavement codes. Henry Charity, mesmerized by Parson's urgency to escape from slavery, reacted by promising to support his courageous quest for liberation from bondage with any means and ways he could.

Jacob Williams, a Survivor of the Nat Turner's Rebellion

In 1864, Jacob managed the three family farm operations, which included tobacco, peanut, and cotton crops. Jacob organized and guided daily farm activities, including slave control, management, training, hiring out, and mating. Caswell Worrell, his nephew, and the overseer helped him by supervising slave labor and other related tasks as directed by Jacob.

As described in David F. Allmendinger, Jr, version of the Southampton Insurrection, the Williams farm in Cross Keys, belongs to three members of the Williams family: to Jacob Williams, to his nephew William Williams, Jr., and to Jacob's sister, Rhoda Worrell. The first of their farms heading toward the Cross Keys, on the north side of the road, belonged to William Jr., son of Jacob's brother Kinchen. A quarter of a mile farther east and across the road to the south stood Jacob's house; and a short walk from there, but still on Jacob's property, near the road, stood his overseer's cabin, occupied by another nephew, Caswell Worrell, the son of Jacob's sister Rhoda Worrell. Caswell's mother had lived on a plot of seventeen acres a short distance east of the cabin, but well south of the road.

Henry Charity knew Jacob Williams was a long-time enslaver in the Cross Keys neighborhood who hired him and other freed people. In 1864, at eighty-four years old, Jacob showed no inclination to change his ways and views. He was quick to judge others based on their appearance, their clothing, speech, and other human traits. He mistreated Black people because he considered them inferior to white people. Henry Charity saw his racist, white supremacy values and politics that characterized him before and after the Civil War. To Jacob, keeping the status quo was the same as supporting law and order. He saw Black people as more violent and dangerous, not disturbed by harsh labor, physical brutality, and not fully human. He received help from institutional racism and promoted racist ideas that boosted him in status above Black people.

Jacob held upholding white supremacy as a justifiable cause for the state to secede and join the

Confederacy at the outbreak of the Civil War. He worried that Parson and his brothers might rebel and self-liberate. As a survivor of the Nat Turner Rebellion, Jacob knew this better than other Southampton slave holders. Jacob used the Bible to justify the economical use of slave labor. He took his subjugation of Parson and other slaves as his natural right. Parson's subordinate position to his relationship with Jacob extended to his relationships with all Southampton white citizens. Jacob mistreated slaves and used fear and violence to control the Black people. As a result, slavery not only broke people's bodies, but it also crushed their spirits. Parson and his brothers worked from dawn to dusk from Monday through Saturday. Sundays were a day to rest and worship. Jacob's farm operations included livestock management, crop cultivation, and other agricultural enterprises. He grew tobacco on his farm, peanuts on his sister's farm, and cotton on his nephew's land.

Jacob's wife, Rachel, headed the domestic labor and supervised Louisa, who did the cooking, cleaning, washing of clothes, food service, and childcare. Louisa, about four and a half feet tall and one hundred pounds in weight, lacked visible interest in political, social, or personal relationships, preferring to be alone. She gave an appearance of being cold or indifferent to others and had little or no interest in men other than Solomon.

Parson disagreed with the ways Jacob subjugated him and sought ways to resist the denial of his basic human rights. Observing the relationship between Jacob and other whites, he conceived the moral principles or norms of human behavior that laws protected as legal rights. To Parson, everyone born on earth inherits human rights that embraced no less than freedom of opinion, expression, thought, and religion. They also included rights to life, rights to education, rights to organize and rights to fair treatment. Absolutely no one in Southampton should be a slave.

Parson and his brothers hated and feared Jacob Williams. They felt he stole labor from them to cultivate the farm and enhance his wealth. To profitably cultivate the land, he needed unpaid slave labor and reasonable liberties, without government interference, to do as he pleased. Parson routinely looked for and found countless acts of resistance to Jacob's domination in the daily farm operations. At its peak, the farm holdings altogether amounted to just twelve slaves, half of whom never belonged to Jacob. He habitually reminded the slaves that they had no value as human beings. He, his family, and the overseer humiliated the slaves as a typical way of life.

Parson believed no one should exist in slavery or servitude, and the Union must abolish enslavement in all its forms and in all places. Fleeing enslavement and running to freedom was a dangerous and potentially life-threatening decision and, if caught by a fugitive slave patrol, it would return him to Jacob Williams, who would then brutally punish him. Because of his fascination with freedom, Parson secretly desired to liberate himself and enlist in the Union Army.

Henry Charity Explained the Two Confiscation Acts

While walking down Meherrin Road after working in Boykins at the railroad company, Parson and his friend Henry Charity found time to discuss the course of the Civil War. They discussed emancipation, the Union Army invasion in nearby Petersburg, defeats of the Confederate armies, and the ongoing Union occupation of Suffolk. In 1864, three million Black people were still in bondage in the states that seceded from the Union, existing without rights and under harsh enslavement laws and oppressive norms.

Parson and Henry Charity also discussed the two Confiscation Acts. Information reached Cross Keys that General Butler declared the fugitive slaves as contraband of war and employed them as laborers. Congress ratified Butler's decision by passing the First Confiscation Act, and the War Department and the Department of the Navy both allowed the employment of confiscated slaves as wage laborers. This was a major first step toward authorizing the Union Army to accept Black volunteers for military service during the Civil War.

Next, they discussed how freeing slaves would deprive the Confederacy of the bulk of its labor force and put public opinion on the Union side. By the summer of 1862, Lincoln realized he could not avoid the slavery question much longer. On July 17, 1862, Congress passed the Second Confiscation Act and the Militia Act, both of which allowed the president to employ Black Americans as workers or soldiers.

Henry Charity informed Parson about the Emancipation Proclamation. On January 1, 1863, United States President Abraham Lincoln signed the

Emancipation Proclamation, freeing slaves in states that had seceded and are part of the Confederacy. It said that all persons held as slaves within any State or designated part of a State, where the people were in rebellion against the United States, are now and forever free.

Parson was glad to learn the proclamation also said that the United States military and naval authority, will recognize and maintain the freedom of such persons, and included the provision for enlisting former slaves into the armed services of the United States, to garrison forts, positions, stations, and other places and to staff vessels of all sorts.

Major General Benjamin F. Butler's Contraband Decision

Growing up in Southampton County, Virginia, in the mid-eighteen hundreds, Parson was afraid to let anyone see him reading. To keep this secret, he collected discarded newspapers from the depot waste container. He learned a great deal about their military and civilian background and retold the stories at family gatherings.

According to Parson, Union Army Major General Benjamin F. Butler, was a shrewd military leader and lawyer, was one of the most controversial men of the American Civil War. Abraham Lincoln appointed him for political reasons, and Butler was the highest-ranking general of volunteers during the war. Using a combination of power, craftiness, and energy, General Butler was a stern but patriotic leader who championed the rights of workers and Black people. In most assignments, he was the right man in the right place at the right time for the job.

After promotion to Major General of Volunteers, the Army transferred and assigned General Butler to command of Fort Monroe, Virginia. Soon, the news reached enslaved people in Southampton County that Butler declined to return to their owner's fugitive slaves who had come within Union lines. He decided that the United States Constitution and the Fugitive Slave Act did not affect another country, which Virginia claimed to be. Enslaved men who found their way to Fort Monroe quickly became known as "contraband," a term that marked their provisional state of being neither free nor enslaved. In later months, the Army adopted "contraband" into common use and signaled changing views of slavery in America. His decision, which came to be known as the "Contraband Decision," enabled thousands of enslaved people from states in rebellion to seek refuge behind Union lines. However, no existing law or policy supported his clever reasoning, which supplied the Union with non-disabled men capable and willing to support the Union. In the following years, Butler's decision had resounding military, political, and social implications as well.

The Union Army occupied New Orleans in the spring of 1862. A joint Union Army and Navy expedition accepted the surrender of New Orleans on April 26, 1862. But the capture of the city and the sealing of the mouth of the Mississippi was just the beginning of the Union Army of occupation. The Army transferred and assigned General Butler, commander of Union troops in occupied New Orleans for seven months, beginning in May 1862.

The Confederate government of Louisiana had formed a militia, including free Black men led by their own officers. This all-Black militia came to General Butler and volunteered to join the Union Army. He transformed the Confederate militia into the First Regiment Native Louisiana Guards, led by Black captains and lieutenants. The men in the regiment came from the New Orleans region. Most were free men of mixed-race whose families the Union government freed when New Orleans became an American possession through the Louisiana Purchase in 1803. These men became members of the first, though unofficial, regiment of Black troops in the Union Army.

General Butler later formed two more Black regiments, commanded by white officers. To keep New Orleans in Union control and bolster troop numbers, on August 22, 1862, Butler issued a general order allowing the enrollment of Black troops. The Black people of New Orleans responded with enthusiasm. Within two weeks, he had enlisted over 1,000 men and formed his first regiment. The general order stipulated only the enrollment of free Black people into the regiment, but the recruiting officers were extremely lax in enforcing this rule, allowing many runaway slaves to enroll with no questions asked.

On September 27, 1862, the regiment officially became the first Black regiment in the Union Army. The First South Carolina Colored Volunteers held the distinction of being the first Black regiment the Union Army organized, but the Union Army had not officially mustered it into service. In August, the War Department ordered Union General Rufus Saxton to organize a regiment of Black soldiers in the South Carolina Sea Islands experimentally. By the end of the year, Saxton had successfully raised the First South Carolina Colored Volunteers, and the regiment took part in raids on the Atlantic Coast.

Taking all of this into account, Major General Butler was a patriotic and skillful administrator who recognized and championed civil-military operations before the Union Army. He was the leader in granting human rights for Black people and their emancipation.

News of the Virginia Peninsula Campaign Reached the County

Parson learned that most of the top Union Army generals were graduates of West Point and were career military officers. In addition, many of them had battlefield experience gained during the Mexican American War. Case in point was Union General George B. McClellan, President Lincoln's first appointee to commander of the Army of the Potomac, the Union's mighty fighting force. In the spring of 1862, news reached in the county that McClellan and Union forces had marched overland to within a few miles of Richmond, the Confederate capital. Parson overheard a lot of chatting in the depot about McClellan's strengths and weaknesses.

General McClellan launched the Peninsula Campaign to capture the Confederate capital of Richmond, Virginia, and bring about a quick end to the Civil War. As retold by Parson, In the Peninsula Campaign, Black people contributed essential human resources and provided intelligence that shaped the campaign's military tactics and strategy, and their activities helped to convince many Northerners that emancipation was a military necessity. The campaign helped lead to the decision to use emancipation to save the Union.

At the start of the war, Lincoln repeatedly insisted that his only war aim was the preservation of the Union. His Republican party aimed for the extinction of slavery but understood that the Constitution protected it in the states where it existed. Therefore, their anti-slavery strategy was to prevent the institution from spreading to the western territories, stop using the government to support the system, and encourage gradual and compensated emancipation. This platform led to Lincoln's 1860 election victory, and he consistently kept this position until the aftermath of the Peninsula Campaign.

General McClellan planned to capture Richmond, Virginia by landing troops at Fort Monroe and attacking northwest up the peninsula formed by the James River and the York River. The campaign involved the largest amphibious operation of the war. On the move northwest up the peninsula towards Richmond, Union troops laid siege to Yorktown for most of April 1862. The siege ended on May 5, 1862, with the Confederate evacuation of Yorktown. Following the surrender of Yorktown, Union forces continued their march northwest towards Richmond, capturing Williamsburg in early May 1862.

Arriving just outside Richmond, the Union forces enjoyed superior numbers, yet during a week of almost continuous fighting, the Confederates used aggressive attacks to drive the Union forces away. But after a week of fierce fighting, McClellan retreated. He thought the enemy had a much larger force. His retreat made Lincoln so mad that he suspended McClellan from command of all the armies, leaving him only the Army of the Potomac.

On August 3, 1862, President Lincoln and General-of-the-Army Henry Halleck ordered McClellan to leave the peninsula and reinforce the Army of Virginia near Manassas Station, Virginia. He defeated Lee at Antietam but lost many men and squandered a chance to crush the Confederate Army. Finally, the exasperated Lincoln fired McClellan.

New in the war was the participation of Black people in ways that were critical to the Union offensive. During the Civil War, reports of slaves fighting alongside their masters shocked Northerners. Reports of slaves' participation contributed to Lincoln's decision to issue the Emancipation Proclamation at the end of that year. As more territory came under Union control, the Union Army's human resource requirements increased and recruiting Black soldiers became a priority for many political and military leaders.

Categorically, General McClellan was a highly intelligent West Point graduate and career military officer. He assessed and planned a plausible army size campaign to capture Richmond, but he was better at managing than leading and failed to accomplish his goal. Unlike General Butler, McClellan opposed the outright abolition of slavery, though he supported the preservation of the Union.

Parson Used His Limited Freedom to Pursue Self-Liberation

In summation, Parson owned and read abolition newspapers, magazines, and pamphlets. This was a great offense. He developed strong opinions about slavery and began discussing human rights and the political implications of the abolition. Parson believed no one should live in slavery or servitude, and that bondage must end in all its forms and places. Because of his fascination with freedom, he secretly desired to liberate himself, enlist in the Union Army and fight for his emancipation.

Contrarily, Jacob supported upholding white supremacy as a justifiable cause for the state to secede and join the Confederate States at the outbreak of the Civil War. He worried that Parson and his brothers might rebel and self-liberate. Parson disagreed with the ways Jacob subjugated him and sought ways to resist the denial of his basic human rights. Observing the relationship between Jacob and other whites, he perceived the moral principles or norms of human behavior that the laws protected as legal rights. To Parson, human rights embraced no less than freedom of opinion, expression, thought and religion, including rights to life, rights to education, rights to organize and rights to fair treatment.

Although General McClellan failed to capture Richmond, Virginia by landing troops at Fort Monroe and attacking northwest up the peninsula, the campaign helped lead to the decision to use emancipation to save the Union. As the war dragged on, Parson took advantage of the chaos of war and used his limited freedom to plan his liberation. He knowingly violated inhumane enslavement codes. And yet, Parson had no shame, guilt, nor regret. He expected that the Civil War outcome would overthrow the status quo by outlawing centuries-old chattel slavery institution.

Last, with nearby infantry skirmishes, cavalry picket activities, and frequent artillery bombardments resounding and raging in the cool fall breeze in Cross Keys, each night at bedtime, Joseph led his younger brothers in prayer.

Chapter Two
Resistance and Abolition

With all its gracious and merciful charm, three major challenges disrupted the status quo of Cross Keys neighbors, all of which affected the county, state, and the nation. The first challenge was the abolishment and the resistance to slavery, banishing the economic and financial cornerstone of the confederacy. The next challenge was the war induced issues of poverty, hunger, and the suffering of soldiers' families and noncombatants, which exemplified the lives of many in Southampton County, long a productive agricultural county. Last, the role Virginia played as the key battleground for the Union's attrition war strategy that led to the extensive physical, moral, and social disruption of its status quo.

Although slavery was the status quo in Virginia for over two hundred years in 1864, its victims still challenged and resisted it daily. Those who found it morally unacceptable fought to abolish it. As the Union Army entered the South, and Black people recognized that freedom was on the horizon, Southampton slaves fled east to army camps and enlisted in the Union Army. This created new separations for some Black families, and subjected women left behind to the abuse of frustrated masters. As the men escaped, women and children eventually followed and helped set up makeshift refugee settlements. Fort Monroe and Camp Craney became settlements where Southampton Black families reunited during the war and the postwar period.

As Southampton slaveholders tighten the grip on their farms, an increasing number of local enslaved men and women still escaped. Parson, driven by his fascination with freedom, secretly desired to liberate himself and enlist in the Union Army. But enslavement meant that it was a crime for him to run away, and he knew if caught by the slave patrollers, they would return him to Jacob Williams, who would then brutally punish him. He discreetly read broadsides about fugitive slaves and abolitionist movement brochures of life outside of enslavement.

Jacob Hired Out Parson to the Boykins Depot

As Parson approached eighteen years old, he recognized that Jacob and the status quo viewed enslaved children as significant assets with a monetary value of their own and as accumulated wealth. Before the Civil War or during ordinary times, Jacob protected and nurtured such assets, if only for economic reasons. Parson, about seventeen years of age, grew and reached the height of five feet eight inches. Remarkably, however, Parson's slavery experiences differed continuously throughout his formative years as he gained physical size, artisan skills, and agricultural experience.

According to Sykes' family chronicles, when not harvesting tobacco, cotton, or peanuts, Jacob hired out Parson to the Boykins Depot to do janitorial work and minor carpentry tasks. Jacob received half a dollar per week and allotted a tiny part to Parson. This was a significant social and economic event for him, and he remembered it throughout the rest of his life.

Parson grew into a charismatic local leader. According to family anecdotes, he lived by his convictions regardless of the obstacles that confronted him. In advocating for self-liberation, he gave insight and clarity to a vision, direction, guidance, coordination, and logistic prudence. Parson motivated potential cohorts by using slavery and oppression as a root cause for self-liberation.

Neighbors in Cross Keys who knew Parson awed his leadership talent. The Black community recognized and appreciated his advocacy, sincerity, and honesty. No one in the Cross Keys ever questioned his integrity. Parson had a deep will to resist to an exceptional degree. He not only lived under the difficulties of personal racism, but more so, the conflicts in a stifling slavery institution that outlawed his freedom and the constant threat of brutal punishment.

As was common in the county, he had a light skin complexion, the offspring of a white slaveholder and his Black female slave. The breeding of enslaved people was a practice extensively in Southampton County after the Union government made it illegal for Americans to engage in the enslavement trade between nations. It included coerced sexual relations between enslaved people. The aim, he learned, was to increase the number of slaves to fill labor shortages without the cost of buying. Regretfully, Parson knew nothing about the ancestry and social history of his parents, Louisa and Solomon. According to laws in Virginia, children of slave women took the status of their mother regardless of the father's identity. This practice and existing laws confined his father's early life and the secrets of miscegenation to the slave quarters.

As the Civil War raged on, Parson devised schemes to undermine the success of the Confederate cause, and to ensure resistance and fulfillment of the abolition movement. He grew into a charismatic, unsung local leader. Freedom gave meaning and joy to his life, and he would not abandon the pursuit of it, knowing the punishment if caught advocating it.

Parson Noticed Francis Hill Toiling in the Fields

Parson hoped the war would abolish slavery in all its hideous forms and in all places. Because of his fascination with freedom, he secretly wanted to liberate himself and enlist in the Union Army. During the Civil War, fearing that Parson and his brothers may well escape, Jacob Williams strengthened the plantation discipline and his grip on the farm. While enslaved Black people fought against the strictures of slavery in their daily lives, another battle was taking place in the public sphere.

Walking back to Cross Keys, Parson noticed a young woman toiling in the fields. She saw him and came closer to the road and smiled at him. Even though the enslavement codes in Southampton County, prohibited for Black men and women to take notice of one another, she attracted him. Her name was Francis Hill, but he thought of her only as a helpless Black woman cursed and abused for being beautiful. For generations, racial oppression included the constant threat of a sexual assault on beautiful Black women. White men raped beautiful Black women just for satisfaction or to enforce their rules of racial dominance and economic hierarchy. They sexually humiliated and assaulted them even in the fields where they toiled and in other open spaces.

Popular judgment in Southampton depicted enslaved women as lustful and promiscuous individuals who tempted white owners into sexual relations, justifying the abuse they perpetrated against Black women. While white women could charge their perpetrators with rape, enslaved Black women had no legal recourse. Their bodies belonged to their owners by code.

Every day after that, Parson and Francis greeted each other with their eyes. He realized he violated the enslavement code, which prohibited Black men from interacting with Black women except for breeding. He broke another enslavement code on the day that he spoke to her. Parson vowed to himself that he would allow no one to put Francis on the auctioning block or into a forced mating for breeding. He did not know how he would prevent it; he knew only that he would.

Parson Devised Forms of Passive Resistance

The form of resistance most feared by Jacob, however, was a violent insurrection, like the resistance led by Nat Turner in which his wife, children and nephew perished. The possibility of a large-scale uprising haunted Jacob, and he publicized his opinions by word of mouth without mentioning the Southampton Insurrection, hoping to increase public vigilance. Word of mouth was the most ubiquitous form of communication during the latter-nineteenth century. Jacob argued for tighter enslavement codes and laws that limited slaves' movements and forms of passive resistance.

Parson and his brothers devised forms of passive resistance, such as damaging equipment, working slowly, and keeping their human rights and religious beliefs alive. In secrecy, they spoke of and shared stories about the popular plots and rebellions that occurred in Virginia. In the brothers' spoken network, stories of cotton field legends, passive forms of resistance, and recitals of renowned insurrections were whistling tones. Parson soon learned that the abolitionists were taking resistance and furthering the abolition battle place into the political sphere.

Henry Charity revealed to Parson a popular story about David Walker, a free Black man born nearby in North Carolina, to a enslaved father and a free Black mother, who wrote and published his brochure, the "Walker's Appeal." In his Appeal, Walker urged slaves to revolt against their masters. As the story went on, he traveled throughout the country before settling in Boston, Massachusetts. He saw the horrors of slavery and joined with other Black activists in the national abolitionism movement. Around 1829, Walker published his Appeal, urging Black people to embrace if necessary armed resistance against whites. His familiarity with Black communication networks helped him distribute his brochure throughout the Confederacy despite white resistance.

As he lay in bed nightly, Parson thought about planning enslavement resistance and an insurrection. He wondered if the distribution of Walker's Appeal inspired the Turner's actions. Was armed resistance justifiable and necessary in the fight for liberty, freedom, and self-determination? How aware was Jacob of the Walker's Appeal and the notion of collusion between the abolitionism movement and enslavement resistances?

Enslavement Resistance and the Abolition Movement

Once the Civil War began, the abolitionists ceased operation of the Underground Railroad as slaves who fled their owners gravitated toward the invading Union forces that came into their vicinity. The enslaved men and women in Southampton County resisted the abhorrence of slavery in their daily lives and crossed the Blackwater River into Union occupied Suffolk. Parson soon learned that abolitionists were continuing resistance and furthering the abolition battle place into the political sphere.

For Parson, deprived of formal education, much of his presence in the public sphere was through word-of-mouth communication and listening to the rhetoric and elocution of local orators. When people gathered for any reason, conversation about the Civil War and the eradication of slavery was a principal pastime. Black people chatted about human rights and freedom, family and separated relatives, past and impending slave auctions, and everything else, from emancipation to self-liberation. Every aspect of the resistance and the abolition movement involved communicating a message, from spirituals directing individual escape plots to weekly newspapers advertising rewards for fugitive slaves.

Henry Charity told Parson stories about the local Quakers, who believed that all people were equal in the eyes of God and spoke out against slavery. In Southampton County, the Reverent David Barrow, a Quaker and pastor of Mill Swamp, Black Creek, and South Quay churches, published an important antislavery brochure and helped to organize the first abolitionist group around 1790. As he also traveled and preached throughout Virginia and North

Carolina, he suffered much persecution. In 1778, at one of his meetings, a gang of twenty men seized, dragged, and forcibly dipped him under water twice, with many jeers and mockeries. In 1798, he left Southampton County and became an advocate for the abolition of slavery in Kentucky.

As he read the old newspapers and brochures that he found, Parson wondered how self-liberation and freedom would look. Over time, he found relevant news and updates about the abolition movement and ongoing resistance by Black people in Southampton County and surrounding counties. From anecdotes told over and over, he grasped that the Nat Turner Insurrection aroused the emancipation debate and gave inspiration to the Abolition Movement. For instance, he learned about William Lloyd Garrison and Arthur Tappan, who in 1833, founded the American Anti-Slavery Society in Philadelphia. Parson learned how they published antislavery newspapers, sponsored speaking tours of Frederick Douglass, and helped form the Underground Railroad.

Before the Underground Railroad ceased operations, thousands of Black people escaped from enslavement to the refuge of Canada. The passage of the Fugitive Slave Act of 1850 that sanctioned the capture and return of escaped slaves anywhere in the United States, spurred migration to Canada. Up to thirty thousand slaves fled to Canada, many free Black people joined to supply them with aid and advice.

The enslaved men and women in Southampton County resisted the abhorrence of slavery in their daily lives and crossed the Blackwater River into Union occupied Suffolk. He used the Southampton soundscape with its warfare-induced ambient noise as a constant reminder to inform, control, and resist oppression. Pervasive sounds, such as soldiers' movement, laborers, wagons, caissons, and animals, meandering about, showed potentially unfavorable situations. One of the more frequent and intense communications of ambient noise came through the boom of artillery in the nearby Petersburg campaign. The cannon and artillery volleys, over thirty miles away, felt like punches to Parson's chest. For him and other enslaved Black people, the sounds were alerts and warnings of trouble and became part of their resistance and abolition tactics. Parson, always, knew that while Jacob was in earshot, silence was a prerequisite for his personal survival.

Parson developed a keen sense of hearing and talent for interpreting the ambient noises that resonated from the soundscape. No sound affected Jacob Williams more than Black people, expressing a growing sense of liberation and freedom. As the war raged on, freed Blacks in Southampton sounded out with public resistance and abolition expression. Black enlistees told anecdotes of how one of the most intimidating weapons they had involved was the sound of their marching. When they announced their arrival with a loud speech, stomping feet, and grinding wheels, the white people in the vicinity reacted with fear. They had never seen nor never expected to see former slaves powerfully and lawfully armed for their overthrow and commanded by invading white officers. Parson was happy to learn that Black soldiers were fighting for the Union.

Railroads Made Possible by Slave Labor

Parson's work experience at the Boykins Depot during his formative years contributed to knowledge of railroad cars, tracks, routes, schedules, as well as the passenger and cargo stops. The railroad brought with it people and commerce, while the depot also served as a hub for moving Confederate troops and supplies. As the railways network grew during the second half of the eighteen-hundreds, the technology of steam locomotion developed as a commercially viable means of transportation in America.

The Seaboard & Roanoke Railroad bridged the Blackwater and Nottoway Rivers and extended its line across the county. It ran from Portsmouth, Virginia, to Weldon, North Carolina. The railroad ran through Southampton County, from the Franklin Depot to and through the Boykins Depot, where it installed a water tank and a wood yard.

Parson enjoyed working at the depot and was fascinated by steam locomotion technology. As reported by the Southeastern Railway Museum, thousands of enslaved Black men worked on the railroad until and during the Civil War. Many southern railroads would hire, rent, or own slaves who would work alongside the paid white laborers. Both slaves and freemen could hold certain positions, including brakeman and firefighter, and others. Usually, the more physically intensive jobs, like track building and maintenance, were entirely the domain of Black men. Laws prevented Black people from holding more skilled jobs, like engineer, though slaves skilled in blacksmithing, masonry, and carpentry worked on the railroads. The pattern of what jobs Black people could hold was set during slavery.

Working as part of the train crew was difficult. Before automatic air brakes and modern couplers, Black people working as brakeman stood a high chance of injury while working on a train. To stop a train, brakemen would hop between the roofs of train cars to apply brakes and could fall off and get crushed. The same was true when coupling cars. When dropping the pin to secure a coupling, any error could cause crushed hands or fingers. Andrew Jackson Beard, a Black man born a slave in Alabama, invented the automatic railroad car coupler, commonly referred to as the "Jenny" coupler. The patent for his invention was issued on November 23, 1897.

In 1869, George Westinghouse invented a railroad braking system using compressed air. The Westinghouse system used a compressor on the locomotive, a reservoir and a special valve on each car, and a single pipe running the length of the train which both refilled the reservoirs and controlled the brakes, allowing the engineer to apply and release the brakes simultaneously on all cars. After the development of knuckle couplers and automatic air brakes, the brakeman's job became much safer, and more attractive to whites. Railroad companies pushed Black people out of these jobs in the late eighteen-hundreds.

The Controversial Nature of Black Military Service

Meanwhile, the War Department issued General Order Number 143 on May 22, 1863, which created the Bureau of Colored Troops, and designated Black regiments as United States Colored Troops, or United States Colored Troops (USCT). Over the course of the next year, the War Department changed the names of black commands. Instead of state designations, they became USCT, and the various units became United States Colored Infantry, Artillery, or Cavalry. The War Department allowed some Black regiments to keep their original state designations. Among these regiments were the 54th Massachusetts Infantry, 55th Massachusetts Infantry, 5th Massachusetts Cavalry, and 29th Connecticut Infantry.

The order directed the Adjutant General to accept Black troops into Union Army companies and afterward, merge the companies into battalions and regiments of Black soldiers. It directed the Army to number the regiments in the order raised. The Adjutant General numerically designated regiments were as, "___Regiment of United States Colored Troops." The Union raised at least 166 regiments of Black soldiers, which fought in approximately 450 combat actions and helped to win the Civil War and the emancipation for their people. The context of the order describing Black men's enlistment showed the War Department's implicit desire to segregate Black troops from the main campaigning regiments of white soldiers.

Because of the controversial nature of black military service, the Lincoln administration decided that the new Black regiments should have white officers. In selected cases, the War Department allowed Black soldiers to serve as chaplains and surgeons. Otherwise, the Lincoln administration barred Black people from the officers' ranks. A major source of controversy for a time was over lower pay Black soldiers received than their white counterparts.

By offering commissions to whites, the War Department hoped to appease objectors in and out of the army. Those whites who endorsed the concept of black military service and helped in its execution could gain commissions or promotions to higher rank. The Department reassured people who opposed the formation of Black regiments that Black people would not hold commissioned rank over white enlistees.

While many officers in the USCT were political appointees, a majority passed an examination. This ensured selectivity and competence among officers of black units that did not exist in white regiments. Most officers of white troops got their commissions through political contacts or election by their comrades. They learned on the job. All officers in the USCT assumed command with knowledge of their duties, which unquestionably aided the development of those units.

Racism was a cause in the decision to commission only white officers. Most white Northerners doubted Black men had the innate ability to fight well and believed that their inferior character would prevent them from becoming obedient soldiers. Some white Northerners viewed service in the USCT as an extension of their prewar antislavery activities, others joined because they wanted to uplift the Black race. Some wanted commissions in the USCT only for the increase in pay and rank. Others, after fighting a couple of years in white units, entered the USCT because they felt this was the best way to contribute to the Union war effort.

Despite the resistance of many whites, the recruitment of Black people into military service went ahead at an almost breathless pace, which produced a new administrative weight that quickly overwhelmed the Adjutant General's Office. To compound these problems, queries for information, requests for appointments to recruit and serve in these new units, mountains of paperwork for enlistees, and orders to organize and equip these commands suffocated its personnel in an avalanche of documents.

The Union Army Fighting Units

During the Civil War, the Union Army had six basic fighting units. The smallest unit was a company, and the largest fighting unit was an army. By joining units together in a stair-step fashion, the Union could form various fighting units of increasing sizes as a regiment, brigade, division, and the corps.

The regiment was the primary fighting unit of the Union Army. A colonel commanded the regiment, each newly formed unit named numerically under Union Army policies and rules governing the designation, classification, and change in status of units. The actual number of men in a regiment varied widely during the war because of personnel losses and gains. A regiment was often composed of men from the same region of a state and often had men who had known each other before the war.

Each newly organized regiment had about 1,000 officers and soldiers. A Union Army regiment included ten companies, each made up of ninety-seven men and three officers. A captain commanded a company, each unit named with the letters A-K. The letter "J" was not used because it looked too much like "I." If the unit had only four to eight companies, the Army called it a battalion rather than a regiment.

Black regiments needed special consideration. The Union government placed unusual demands on its officers and men and more carefully supervised the recruitment process. In the Union, state governments had a hand in creating new regiments. Most of the black units, however, would have ex-slaves as their enlistees, and they came from seceding states. The Union government directed the recruitment of those black units.

In the Union Army, an average of four regiments joined to make a brigade. This size unit had approximately 4,000 men and a brigadier general commanded it. Union brigades named with numbers. To organize a division, the

Union Army joined three to five brigades. A division had approximately 12,000 men, and a major general commanded it. During the war, a Union Army corps could have between two and four divisions, but most often had up to three. The Union Army named corps in series beginning with Roman numeral "I." A major general commanded a corps. An army included from one to eight corps and a general commanded it.

On May 15, 1864, the first Black troops that fought General Robert E. Lee's Army of Northern Virginia, was the 23rd Regiment of the United States Colored Troops. During the Battle of Spotsylvania Court House, the second major engagement in Lieutenant General Ulysses S. Grant's Overland Campaign, a major Union offensive chased down Robert E. Lee, destroyed his forces, and defeated the Confederates. The battle gained a lot of respect from the white troops who cheered the Black troops' actions. It proved to the white soldiers that Black people would fight when given the opportunity.

Lieutenant General Ulysses S. Grant, the Second Three-Star General

Parson was glad to read that President Abraham Lincoln promoted Ulysses S. Grant to Lieutenant General after his victory at Chattanooga. A graduate of West Point, Grant distinguished himself as a daring and competent soldier during the Mexican - American War. While it motivated Parson, President Lincoln's next appointee to commander of the Army of the Potomac gave Jacob the feeling that the end of the Confederacy was near. For the next thirteen months, Union General Grant fought Robert E. Lee during the high-casualty Overland Campaign and at Petersburg.

On March 9, 1864, President Abraham Lincoln officially commissioned General Ulysses S. Grant as Lieutenant General in the Regular Army of the United States. Only George Washington had risen to that rank in the United States Army before him. Grant was characteristically humble. In addition, he would also become the fifth General-in-Chief in the Army's history. Throughout its forty-three-year existence, this demanding role had stressed and exasperated its occupants like few other jobs could. The next day, he assumed command of the armies of the United States.

Within the Army, Grant's personality, rank, and record of success instantly enabled him to exercise the power entrusted as Lieutenant General in the Army of the United States. He had the full trust of his two principal field commanders, Major Generals William Tecumseh Sherman, and General George G. Meade. They not only respected his rank and position but also had full confidence in his character and military judgment. There would be none of the grudging acceptance of orders or schemes to circumvent the General-in-Chief's authority that had plagued General Halleck.

Congress did not clearly outline the General-in-Chief's powers and responsibilities. Grant did not enjoy complete liberty in managing the war, but neither was he stuck in the role of an adviser to the president. He understood that his promotion brought with it the expectation that he would exercise his office in the field and solve the previously unsolvable problem of Robert E. Lee. Out in the field, Grant realized he would be free to command as he saw fit. His political savvy included his accepting Lincoln's insistence that politically influential men such as

Major Generals Benjamin Butler, Franz Sigel, and Nathaniel Banks receive important commands, listening respectfully to Lincoln's suggestions, and making Lincoln feel welcome whenever he visited headquarters.

Grant led the Union war effort from here for the last year of the war. From his tent, and then cabin, overlooking the rivers, he issued orders and coordinated movements of the Union armies throughout the nation to defeat the South. While General Philip H. Sheridan battled Confederate forces in the Shenandoah Valley and General William T. Sherman marched across Georgia and up through the Carolinas, Grant intensified his grip on Petersburg. While running the war, Grant received many notable political and military visitors at his headquarters.

In the spring of 1864, after leading the Army of the Potomac through the Overland Campaign from the Wilderness to Cold Harbor, Lieutenant General Ulysses S. Grant transferred the army to the south side of the James River to seize the Confederate supply hub in Petersburg. When four days of bloody frontal assaults did not capture the city, he ordered the army to begin siege operations against it. On May 5, 1864, the 1st and 22nd USCT Regiments arrived at City Point, and during the first weeks of occupation, bolstered their ranks by recruiting runaway slaves. Prior to the siege, the railroad connected City Point to Petersburg. Its strategic position, next to a torn-up railroad bed and the rivers, offered Grant easy access to points along the front, as well as good transportation and communications with Fort Monroe, Virginia, and Washington, D.C., in the rear. Through the hard work of soldiers in 1st and 22nd USCT Regiments and civilians, including former slaves, they constructed twenty-one miles of a military railroad by March 1865, linking

City Point to the Union front lines around Petersburg and supplying over 100,000 troops.

On June 15, 1864, Grant set up his field headquarters at City Point, Virginia, staying there for the next nine and one-half months. Living in tents during the summer and a two-room log cabin during the winter, Grant directed most of the last months of the war from City Point, eight miles behind the siege lines east of Petersburg. General Ulysses S. Grant's failure to capture Richmond or destroy the Confederate Army of Northern Virginia during the Overland Campaign caused him to cast his glance toward Petersburg. Capturing this important transportation hub would isolate the Confederate capital and force General Robert E. Lee to either evacuate Richmond or fight the numerically superior Grant on open ground. By the morning of June 15, Grant was ready to launch his attack.

Commencement of the Petersburg Campaign

With his inability to capture Richmond or destroy the Confederate Army of Northern Virginia during the Overland Campaign, General Grant moved his army across the James River and to the city of Petersburg, about twenty miles south of Richmond. Confederate General Pierre Gustave Toutant Beauregard defended the city of Petersburg with a small division of the Confederate army.

General Grant's strategic goals shifted from the defeat of General Robert E. Lee's army in the field to cutting off the supply and communication routes to the Confederate capital at Richmond. Petersburg was at the junction of three railroads that supplied General Lee's army, as well as to Richmond. For these reasons, General Grant resolved to destroy the railroads, to capture the city, and put an end to the Confederates' source of supplies. General Lee was aware of these venerable conditions and situations. In response, Lee resolved to defend Petersburg to save it from capture if possible, and thus began the Petersburg Campaign.

Grant relayed the war plan to his field commanders, General Meade, and General Butler. While the Army of the Potomac, commanded by General Meade, advanced on the capital from the north. The Army of the James, commanded by General Butler, would advance from the south, up the James River. General Grant charged General Butler with cutting General Lee's supply line, the Richmond, and Petersburg Railroad, forcing Lee to move troops to the south and weakening his defense against Grant and Meade.

From June 15-17, 1864, the outnumbered Confederate forces saved Petersburg from Union capture with powerful fortifications and reinforcements from Lee's Army of Northern Virginia. After four days of fighting with no success, Grant began siege operations. Grant's strategy was to surround Petersburg and cut off Lee's supply route to the south. As he attacked Petersburg, other Union troops simultaneously attacked around Richmond, which would strain the Confederacy to the breaking point. During the ten months of the siege, both armies endured skirmishing, mortar and artillery fire, poor rations, and intense boredom. It would be 291 days before the United States flag would fly over Petersburg again.

Parson Hoped to Liberate Himself from Racial Oppression

To surmise, Jacob feared that Parson and the other slaves might escape, tightened the discipline and grip on his farm. During the Civil War, many southern railroads would hire, rent, or own slaves who replaced white laborers conscripted into confederate military service. Jacob hired out Parson to the Boykins Depot. For abolitionists, the Civil War was the culmination of a decades-long struggle for the slave's freedom. With implementing the Emancipation Proclamation on January 1, 1863, the abolition movement reached a higher level in the political sphere.

Parson, a man of unbending independence, hoped to self-liberate himself and live free, equal, and prosperous in Southampton. The enslaved people in Southampton County resisted the abhorrence of slavery in their daily lives and crossed the Blackwater River into Suffolk. When the abolitionists stopped the use of the Underground Railroad, Southampton slaves fled east toward the Union forces controlling and occupying nearby territories.

Racial oppression included the constant threat of a sexual assault on beautiful Black women. Parson's brief first encounter with Frances Hill was a wake up call for him. When they greeted each other, he realized he violated the enslavement code, which prohibited Black men from interacting with Black women except for breeding. Irrespective of the enslavement code, which prohibited him from interacting with Francis, Parson vowed to himself to protect and liberate her. Jacob wanted tighter enslavement codes and laws that prohibited Black men from espousing Black women.

Finally, Virginia played the key battleground for the Union's war strategy to capture the Confederate capital of Richmond, Virginia, and bring an end to the Civil War. Grant's tactical plan was to surround Petersburg and end the Confederates' source of supplies, which led to the extensive physical, moral and social disruption of the state.

Chapter Three
Commitment to Self-Liberation

The long struggle to abolish human bondage was one of the great moral movements in American history. Further, its success resulted from the commitment of Black people to self-liberation and agitation by their allied organizations. As the Civil War dragged on, the Union came to realize the strategic advantages of emancipation. Hundreds of enslaved men, women, and children took flight from Southampton County east toward the Virginia Peninsula. The occupying Union forces in neighboring Nansemond and Norfolk counties became the physical envisioning of President Lincoln's Emancipation Proclamation. Lincoln saw that arming Black men was not a question of sentiment or taste, but one of physical force. The liberation of millions of enslaved people shut down a major part of the confederacy labor force and strengthened the Union forces with an influx of human resources.

In the conflict's waning days, Parson tried to deepen his knowledge and appreciation of emancipation, agricultural commerce, information technology, and warfare between the states through observation of his surroundings. A gifted thinker, he surmised that information was the equalizer of the hindrances and opponents of his journey to liberate himself from enslavement and racial oppression. He gathered information to help fulfill his commitment to self-liberation and emancipation by meandering along southeastern Virginia swamps, waterways, and railways to freedom.

Union forces, abolition orators, public discourse, and printed material helped him pursue and achieve his commitment to self-liberation. He saw how the war changed the lives of the slaves, soldiers, and civilians in Southampton County. He soon recognized the crucial connections between democracy, humanity, politics, and the economy with the ending of Black citizens' enslavement. Parson's utmost desire was the end of chattel slavery and racial oppression. A man of unbending independence, Parson sternly committed himself to self-liberation and emancipation.

Parson followed the major Civil War engagements and other crucial issues by examining discarded maps, brochures, and newspapers. From his observations, Parson grasped the fundamentals of human rights that characterized human conduct and protected the civil and legal rights of free people with local, state, and national laws. Parson gained an appreciation of the strategies and tactics for slavery resistance, as well as the moral justifications and motivation of the abolition movement. As a result, he became more committed to self-liberation and fleeing enslavement. He learned that hundreds of slaves in Southampton County had abandoned their bondage in pursuit of freedom. At every opportunity, he roamed through the trash bins in the depot, looking for and garnering documents about resistance and abolition. He did not understand all the written topics, but he examined them and soon embraced the fundamentals of human rights, including the right to life, right to education, right to organize and fair treatment, among other principles.

Parson Prepared for the Self-Liberation Quest

Parson found the discarded maps, pamphlets, and periodicals very helpful in planning his liberation quest. In his haven, he risked life and limb to guard and protect his collection of documents about freedom, abolitionists, resistance, and humanity. His emerging understanding of human rights helped him to envision a new future and life after emancipation. He believed that the best way to learn was to find and observe winning behavior, escape and evasion methods, and various tactical models.

According to Sykes' family chronicles, about age seventeen, Parson's primary labor revolved entirely around the cultivation and production of tobacco, a very labor-intensive process. He grew up and came of age cultivating tobacco on the Williams' farm. Often, he fantasized about owning a commercial tobacco venture that employed paid labor rather than enslaved people. Regrettably, enslavement codes restricted the rights of enslaved people to buy, sell, and own a commercial venture.

As he grew older, Parson had a lot less personal life and worked much more on the Williams' farm from dawn to well after dusk six days a week. After twelve to fifteen hours of work in a day, he could return to the cabin he shared with his brothers. When in proximity to Jacob, he followed the deeply fixed white superiority-black subordination protocol. He pretended to show little or no appreciation of his self-esteem, resistance, or self-liberation concepts. When engaged socially alone in their cabin, the brothers engaged in discussions of enslavement resistance, human rights, and self-determination. Jacob treated Parson and his brothers as property and inflicted genocidal-like hardship on them.

Parson had the unique ability to keep and recite the political, economic, and social information he learned and shared it with other enslaved people. Eventually, he learned that slavery was a commercial venture that existed where it was economically viable for those in power. Jacob Williams found slavery profitable and enjoyed the rate of return on slaves comparable to his other assets.

Parson urgently wanted to liberate himself and to learn as much as he could from other enslaved people who conducted successful escapes. He continued to gain height, weight, muscle mass, and body hair while developing the ability to think through his ideas and articulate his thoughts. Further, he paid close attention to the political, economic, and social events that he saw, read, and overheard. He displayed knowledge of things, places, and people with which he had no direct experience.

In his haven, Parson studied oft recited daring escapes from slavery and applied them to his quest by planning and preparing for his liberation. Parson's covert explorations went undetected for two years and followed the course of the Civil War and other political, economic, and social events. Away from his haven, he deliberately refrained from reading in front of others, because having that knowledge put him at risk of punishment. Through observation and examining his cache of printed material, Parson learned about the invention of the printing press that brought newspapers to the masses. The invention of the telegraph produced rapid communication; the railroad enhanced mobility, and the development of economies of scale gave fortune and power to men of a segregated social, economic, and political class. He kept and extended the information he learned by examining others. Parson practiced the positive things he saw to improve and advance his behavior and personal skills.

On the west bank of the Blackwater River, people in the defensive line, where Confederate soldiers encamped, picketed, and marched through, had to deal with hardships such as food shortage, lack of farm supplies, pillaging, and insufficient information about loved ones who escaped from slavery. Parson equipped himself with the survival skills and habits he needed for self-liberation through intense observation of his surrounding and listening to the soundscape. His covert reading and observation of the Civil War era transportation, communication and technology advances had a profound effect on him. He redundantly read about the moral principles and human rights that described certain norms of human behavior and of the missing or unimplemented processes for local, state, and national laws to protect and assure freed Black citizens of their civil and legal rights. Parson became more and more committed to self-liberation and escaping enslavement. Based on his observations and surroundings, he created a mental map to follow in pursuit of his self-liberation quest.

Parson Studied Jacob's Process for Marketing and Selling Tobacco

While risky throughout the war, the Southampton County economic process for marketing and selling tobacco grew markedly worse in 1864 after President Lincoln issued the Emancipation Proclamation. Parson wanted to understand how he could use the process to defend human rights, pursue self-liberation, promote economic development, and self-determination. Tobacco manufacture played an important economic, political, and diplomatic role in Virginia during the Civil War.

In early August 1864, Jacob began harvesting his tobacco crop from which Parson gained valuable economic knowledge that helped in his liberation quest. The Boykins Depot created a link for shipments of tobacco and other products originating along the Roanoke River and its canal system from points west to reach port facilities in the Norfolk area on the harbor of Hampton Roads. During the Civil War, Norfolk and Portsmouth competed with Petersburg, Virginia, which had access to the navigable part of the James River at City Point via the Appomattox River for rail service from its south and west.

According to Sykes' family chronicles on Parson, the process for marketing and selling tobacco was a complex business venture that included a variety of steps. Warehouse operators in the county created competitive auctions, where Jacob and other farmers displayed their crops to different buyers and to get the best bid. Parson scrutinized the commercial process and learned from his experience as Jacob's coachman, the primary steps for buying and selling tobacco.

Parson and his brothers started harvesting tobacco in early August and into early fall. To harvest the plants, he took the leaves as they ripened, grabbed the stem closest to the plant, and with a little twist, pulled it off the plant. Next, he tucked the leaf under his arm. When his arm became full of leaves, he took it to a wooden trailer on sled runners that a mule would pull. Once he filled the entire sled, the mule pulled it up to the curing barn. Parson scrutinized the graded tobacco, tied it into bundles, and got it ready for the market.

After harvesting the tobacco, the brothers dried, cured, and ripened the leaves. Around the time of harvest, the tobacco plants were about five feet tall and grew on individual main stalks. Parson learned firsthand the ordeals of cultivating tobacco, the challenging work and degradation, the body weakened by fatigue and hunger, and frequent farm injuries. Parson noticed the way Jacob keenly managed harvesting, curing, and selling tobacco from his farm to the market. As the number-one cash crop for the county, cultivating tobacco was the way Jacob made money to live on.

In Southampton, tobacco buyers and certifiers set up inspection stations with warehouses for hosting auctions in Boykins. At the market, Jacob waited for the tobacco buyers to come through and tell him what they had graded his harvest. The auctioneers walked down the rows. chanted prices and urged buyers to bid for each pile. Jacob was at their mercy. Whatever they told him they could give, that was what he had to take.

The tobacco business process amazed Parson. Riding back to the farm with Jacob, he reminisced about watching the buyers visit the inspection stations and examine the tobacco before buying certificates. As buyers looked to find high-quality tobacco, Jacob sought a premium in price. When he had a good sale, he was happy. The warehouse operators and buyers were happy, but the enslaved people felt deprived. Parson clearly learned by observing Jacob's behavior why he hungered for free Black labor and drove enslaved people relentlessly to toil on his farm.

Parson and his brothers learned early that successful tobacco farming in Southampton County was the product of its soils, transportation facilities, and its waterways. When not farming, Jacob hired out Parson to the Boykins Depot. By observing daily events and listening to conversations in Railroad Depot, he learned more and more about people, places, and things that he had no firsthand experience with. He gained helpful economic expertise to prepare for and survive after his self-liberation quest.

Parson Learned the Power of Telegraph

Since 1861, the emancipation both enraged the Confederacy with its promise of freedom for their slaves and threatened the very existence of the Confederate States of America. While working at the Boykins Depot, Parson learned the mysterious power of the telegraph system and how it made information available everywhere to anybody. As he secretly watched and listened to telegraph workers, Parson soon learned that the telegraph was a valuable communication device used by civilians in commerce, for government endeavors, and as a military service medium. It helped field commanders to direct real-time battlefield operations and allowed senior military officials to coordinate strategy across enormous distances. On Thursday, January 1, 1863, the transmission of the Emancipation Proclamation text over the telegraph began, infuriating the Confederacy.

Information is knowledge of something learned from somewhere else. The telegraph system made knowledge available everywhere to anyone. During the Civil War, the telegraph was the great equalizer that dramatically improved the quality of life through the click of a telegraph key. It developed as a potential way to rid enslavement and racial oppression because of social characteristics, geographic location, physical or sensory abilities. Once the war started, the telegraph ensured that Americans would have much better access to war information.

There are many examples of how the telegraph leveled the playing field and opened doors for all citizens. For example, during the Civil War, hundreds of reporters from Union and Confederate newspapers published stories from battles on land and sea. Only one of those reporters was Black, Thomas Morris Chester, was the nation's first Black war correspondent. The correspondents filing those front-line stories that shaped Americans' perceptions about the war were mostly white men telegraphing the conflict primarily through the lens of other white men and their families. Theirs were the only perspectives conveyed in the mainstream press until the Philadelphia Press hired Chester to cover the Black troops in Virginia.

Writing under the pseudonym Rollin, the thirty-year-old Harrisburg, Pennsylvania native whose mother had escaped slavery, became the first and only African American correspondent during the war for a major newspaper. Embedded with the United States Colored Troops in the Army of the James from August 1864 until June 1865, Chester, who had recruited Black men to the Union Army, gave voice and dignity to the Black soldiers struggling for their right to fight, for parity with white troops and respectful treatment. According to published reports, he wrote in the Philadelphia Press of Black troops, "Every man looked like a soldier, while inflexible determination depicted upon every countenance." Chester knew how to frame the plight of all Black people in the war's context and the troops fighting for their freedom.

Self-liberation was a process and emancipation a contested claim, as reflected by the protracted struggle over how American life would change without slavery. Technological advances helped Parson in his preparations for self-liberation, along with his knowledge of resistance and abolition movement, and learning about the growth of the feminist movements. He committed himself to understanding this technology, even though it meant going against everything Jacob Williams taught him to know, behave, and believe.

Parson learned and recognized the power of the telegraph and the benefits of rapid information in promoting liberation and freedom. He longed to understand how he could use it to support human rights, pursue self-liberation, promote economic development, and self-determination.

Lincoln Opened the White House to Black Americans

Between 1862 and 1865, Lincoln opened the White House to Black people in ways that would have been unthinkable before. Black men and women entered the Executive Mansion for public receptions and private meetings. Some joined Abraham and Mary Lincoln for tea. Others boldly petitioned for equality and political rights. Some came by the invitation of the President. Others walked through the White House gates uninvited and unannounced. Some offered their services to the Union Army. Others called on Lincoln to ensure that the Union's Colored Troops received equal treatment.

According to the Library of Congress Archives, at the beginning of the Civil War, Lincoln had rejected Black volunteers, in part because he had no confidence they would fight well. In the ensuing months and years, arguments by

Black Americans who visited the President and his willingness to listen shaped Lincoln's thinking and sentiments about emancipation and racial equality. Black Americans, from Robert Smalls to Frederick Douglass, visited and had personal interactions and discussions with President Lincoln.

According to an era news report, Robert Smalls traveled to Washington, D. C., where he met Lincoln at the White House. It was the most consequential meeting Lincoln had with a Black person in the first two years of his administration, a critical period in Lincoln's developing policy on Black citizenship. Parson heard how Smalls secured his own liberty with stealth and bravery. Before dawn on May 13, 1862, Smalls took command of a Confederate steamer and steered it out of Charleston Harbor. The twenty-three-year-old, who had worked as a slave aboard the vessel, brought fifteen other enslaved people with him, including his wife and two young children. During Smalls' meeting with Lincoln, he urged the president to allow Black men to join the Union Army. After meeting Smalls, Lincoln finally embraced the idea of enlisting Black troops. Smalls left Washington, D. C., bearing a letter from the War Department that allowed the raising of Black volunteers in South Carolina.

Frederick Douglass' first meeting with Lincoln, in August 1863, was to protest discrimination against Black soldiers serving in the Union Army. From Douglass' newspaper the North Star, and his autobiography, Parson learned the important fundamental of human rights. He read about Douglass' daring escape from slavery and courageous quest for his liberation from bondage. Parson agreed with Douglass' stance on woman's rights and how he underwent an evolution of his views on human rights. Suffrage, some felt, was a controversial issue that would alienate men from supporting the more palatable planks of the woman's rights platform. Douglass' second meeting, which Lincoln started, concerned the President's 1864 re-election campaign and Douglass' views on human rights. Frederick Douglass believed Black Americans could achieve freedom and full citizenship only by taking part in the war.

As Union forces penetrated the Virginia peninsular, multitudes of slaves fell into their hands for safety. Eager recruiters greeted formerly enslaved people as they entered Union camps. The military service of Black soldiers was essential to winning the civil war. Within those occupied areas where enslaved people used the Army as their shield to freedom, the Union forces got enough Black recruits to fill several regiments.

Grant Launched the Union Forces' Petersburg Offensives

On June 9, 1864, to support Grant's 1864 Overland Campaign, Major General Benjamin Butler sent 4,500 men from his forces in Bermuda Hundred to cross the Appomattox River and capture Petersburg. A Confederate militia, comprising teenagers and overage men with some recovering wounded soldiers from the hospital, halted the major attack by Union cavalry up the Jerusalem Plank Road. The militia took heavy losses but held up the Union forces until Confederate reinforcements sent by Lieutenant General Pierre G. T. Beauregard arrived to turn back the attackers.

On June 15, 1864, Lieutenant General Grant began his assaults on Petersburg, usually striking simultaneously from positions north and south of the James River. In June and July, he launched the Union forces' first, second, and third Petersburg offensives. Next, in August, September, and October 1864, he launched his fourth, fifth, and sixth Petersburg offensives. Finally, in August, September, and October, Grant launched the Union forces' seventh, eighth, and ninth Petersburg offensives. The Union Army held the strategic initiative during the entire operation, launching two-pronged attacks, supported by several cavalry and infantry raids. Under Grant's leadership, the initial Union advances against Petersburg promised success.

Grant began the assault on Petersburg by having Butler repeat the June 9 attack with much larger numbers. The leading elements of the Union attack included Major General William F. Smith's XVIII Corps, aided by Brigadier General August V. Kautz's cavalry division. The 16,000 soldiers Butler commanded outnumbered General P. G. T. Beauregard's estimated 5,400 Confederate defenders.

During the next three days, the entire Army of the Potomac, along with much of Major General Benjamin F. Butler's Army of the James, appeared in front of Beauregard's lines and lunged forward in a series of bloody, uncoordinated assaults. Beauregard fended off these attacks on the one hand while writing urgent messages to Lee on the other, imploring the Army of Northern Virginia to send help to Petersburg. Lee gradually responded, and by June 18 his entire force had taken position behind the second makeshift line Beauregard had erected during the previous seventy-two hours. The presence of Lee's army ended Grant's prospects for quickly capturing Petersburg.

Confederate defenders called upon enslaved and free Black people to construct breastworks that impeded the advance of the Union Army, particularly at the beginning of the war in eastern and later in central Virginia. The Confederate army forced thousands of Black Americans to support their defensive operations as teamsters, cooks, body servants, and laborers. They impressed 1,200 slaves and free Black people to work on a ten-mile-long semicircle of fifty-five artillery strong points with both flanks anchored on the Appomattox River defensive line. Having lost almost 11,400 men in four days against a Confederate loss of 4,000, Grant called off the assaults and ordered the Union forces to dig in.

Army of the James Boost Its Ranks of USCT Regiments

General Benjamin Butler and his unit commanders in the Army of the James, sent raiding parties beyond their fortified lines to find Black recruits to bolster the ranks of the USCT regiments, 35th Regiment USCT, 36th Regiment USCT, 37th Regiment USCT, and 14th United States Colored Heavy Artillery. The regiments included free men, formerly enslaved people, contraband and white officers from the United States and abroad. The Federal Bureau of Colored Troops organized the units at Camp Hamilton, Virginia, in 1863, and attached them to Fortress Monroe, Virginia, in 1864.

As recruiting began, the War Department centralized the organization of its Black regiments under the Federal Bureau for Colored Troops led by Major Charles W. Foster. Parson learned that Henry Charity and his three brothers enlisted in cavalry units. Henry Charity enlisted in Company E, First Cavalry Regiment, United States Colored Troops;

Joshua Charity, Company A, First Cavalry Regiment, United States Colored Troops; Thomas Charity, Company E, First Cavalry Regiment, United States Colored Troops; and Friday Charity in Company I, 2nd United States Colored Cavalry. On May 5, 1864, Black soldiers in the 36th and 37th USCT Infantry regiments seized the Union complex at City Point, situated where the James and Appomattox Rivers meet. According to the news report, the two regiments, previously mustered into service as the 1st and 2nd North Carolina Colored Infantry and were in southeastern Virginia when the Federal Bureau of Colored Troops changed their designations.

Lieutenant General Grant employed USCT regiments in all nine distinct offensives at Petersburg, usually striking simultaneously north and south of the James River. From June 15-18, 1864, he attacked on the eastern Petersburg defenses force back toward the city. The 2nd United States Colored Cavalry fought on the Petersburg front, as did Battery B of the 2nd United States Colored Artillery, the 10th United States Colored Infantry, the 23rd United States Colored Infantry, and the 38th United States Colored Infantry Regiments.

Parson Grew Committed to Self-Liberation and Emancipation

Parson eventually learned that slavery was a commercial venture that existed where it was economically viable for those in power. Jacob Williams found slavery profitable and enjoyed the rate of return on slaves comparable to his other assets. Parson urgently wanted to liberate himself and to learn as much as he could from other enslaved people who conducted successful escapes. He gained helpful economic expertise to prepare for and survive after his self-liberation quest.

The tobacco business process amazed Parson. Parson clearly learned by observing Jacob's behavior, and why he hungered for free Black labor and drove enslaved people relentlessly to toil on his farm. Parson learned and recognized the power of the telegraph and the benefits of rapid information in promoting liberation and freedom. From telegraph transmissions, he learned more and more about people, places, and things that he had no firsthand experience.

Parson learned that the liberation of millions of enslaved Black men, women, and children shut down a major part of the confederacy labor force and strengthened the Union forces with an influx of human resources. According to the telegraph report, he also learned that President Lincoln opened the White House to Black Americans. To come to the point, Parson and his enslaved brothers grew dedicated to Self-Liberation and learned to avoid contribution to the confederate war effort in diverse ways and repelled genocidal-like hardship. They undermined Jacob's commercial tobacco venture as they committed to self-liberation and emancipation.

Chapter Four
Reactions to and Reflections on Freedom

Since June 1864, the bombardment of Petersburg dominated the soundscape in the Cross Keys. On reflecting and reacting to the nearby fighting, Parson thought about his quest for liberation, hopefully manifested in the three-year-old armed conflict, as a way toward achieving President Lincoln's grand objectives. For months now, Parson and his brothers have listened to the roaring soundscape filled with artillery, cavalry, and infantry forces clashing in and around Petersburg. Parson hoped the outcome of the nearby combat would overthrow the status quo by outlawing the centuries-old chattel slavery institution. The cruel treatment he received from Jacob varied, but the laws in Virginia left Parson with hardly any defense or recourse. To reassert his dominance over Parson, he meted out harsh punishment in response to disobedience or other perceived infractions of rebellion. In Southampton, he and other slaveholders were free to whip, shackle, hang, beat, burn, mutilate, brand, and imprison slaves. More hideous, they could and often subjected enslaved Black women to rape and sexual abuse.

As Parson reflected on his life, he recognized this and believed that Black citizens in Cross Keys had a natural urge to be free and fight to determine their own lives. By observation and comparison of his surroundings, Parson grasped the injustice of his enslavement and felt called to react against slavery for no other reason than to gain his freedom. He learned enslaved African descendants had always desired freedom and self-liberation was the best method to gain it. As he became more committed to his quest for self-liberation, Parson was unconcerned about the discouragement and negative opinions of others. When Parson's aims were under attack, like any self-driven person, his creative mental talents took control.

As he grew into adulthood, Parson began understanding the moral, political, and economic issues that led to the war. The Civil War erupted from a variety of long-standing disputes and disagreements about the American way of life and social affairs. For a century, the people and politicians of the northern and southern states had been clashing over the issues that had finally transformed into war causes. People in the Union came to view enslavement as not just socially unjust, but morally wrong. People in the Confederacy argued for greater rights for the states and others argued that the Union government needed to have more control.

As Parson reflected on American life and politics, he grew empathetic toward abolitionists and against enslavement and enslavers. He recognized the economic disparity that led to irreconcilable differences in societal and political views. As he grew older, Parson realized the need for at least some outside help on how to escape and who to trust as cohorts. Parson learned to cultivate strong relationships with other people and recognized how important friendships were. He knew the Southampton landscape inside and out. In addition, he knew the beginning and end of various pig paths that meandered throughout the county. Most important, he knew that the Blackwater River ran north-south through the county and east of the river was Union occupied territory.

Issues that Sparked the Call for Self-Liberation

Parson put no place, no limits on his skills and abilities or what he or other Black people could do or achieve. Reasoning and planning skills came naturally to Parson not through aggressively seeking it, but because of the moral, economic, and political crisis during the prime of his life. He was obviously well organized, self-disciplined, keenly focused, and driven. Through observation and examining his cache of printed material, Parson realized the inequalities in a patriarchal social class.

Amazingly, Parson enhanced his reading skills and could read and understand the scrounged information. Parson practiced the positive things he observed to improve and advance his behavior and personal skills. He cultivated a behavior; that was reactive and reflective of the positive things he learned through his accumulated experience. The newly cultivated behavior descended from generation to generation. Parson's desire to run away came from the information he collected by observing the behavior of people who lived and mingled freely. He developed a practical picture of the inhumanity and injustice of enslavement. From the harsh upbringing on Jacob's farm, the call for self-liberation sparked naturally in Parson.

Parson saw the big picture rather than seeing things in minor details and took the time to listen to his brothers' concerns. As he grew, Parson learned that as a slave, he had no rights. Jacob Williams and his family had extensive, unchecked power over him and their other slaves. He socially and economically depended on slave labor for the family's survival and prosperity.

Parson found discarded maps, pamphlets, and periodicals helpful in planning his liberation quest. In his haven, he risked life and limb to guard and protect his collection of documents about freedom, abolitionists, resistance, and humanity. Further, he grasped the injustice of his enslavement and felt called to react against slavery for no other reason than to gain his freedom. He learned that enslaved African descendants had always desired freedom and self-liberation was one of the best methods to gain it. The inhumane laws and enslavement codes in Virginia left Black people without defense or recourse.

Parson Observed how to Produce and Market Cotton

Union naval blockades and invasions into the South hampered Southampton County cotton growers' ability to sell their products overseas. Union forces destroyed, disrupted, or captured Southern transportation and manufacturing facilities. Before the war started, cotton plantations were very profitable, and Jacob Williams could get large tracts of land for little money. Jacob depended on slave labor that could not resign or demand wages to cultivate and harvest his cotton crop. As the cotton economy became more profitable, Virginia enforced enslavement codes restricting the trade and commerce rights of Black people to buy, sell, and produce their own cotton.

At the time of the Civil War, cotton had become the most valuable crop of the Confederacy and played a vital role in the conflict. Parson keenly observed the cultivation, production, and the marketing of cotton, the most valuable crop of Southampton County and, before the war, a major export commodity from the United States. Cotton was the principal crop of Jacob's operation and the fulcrum of Black enslavement's profitability. The war disrupted both the production and the marketing of what Jacob hoped would be the financial basis of his farm. However, the Union's blockades stalled not only the cotton economy but also the foreign relations of the Confederacy.

By late September 1864, Southampton County was running out of everything, including men, equipment, money, and food. Jacob operated on credit and needed money to settle debts that were due. His Confederate taxes also were in arrears, and the plantation needed food and other goods, as well as supplies for the next year's production. Jacob assigned Parson to help his brother Henry deliver wagon loads of cotton to the local merchants, who represented distant buyers with setups in Boykins Depot. The trips gave the brothers time to reflect on relationships between enslaved men and women. They talked about the abhorrence of slavery in Southampton, reflected on the abolitionist movement, and organizing a self-liberation journey. They discussed and exchanged information about recent escapes from the enslavement in the Cross Keys.

According to often recited anecdotes, Parson and his brothers learned to avoid contributing to the confederate war effort in diverse ways and on their own terms. Through subtle disobedience, work slowdowns, and other covert operations of rebellion, they undermined Jacob's commercial venture and promoted their self-liberation quest to be slaves no more. The methods and tactics varied, but their goal remained unchanged: liberation and equality. For Parson, the Civil War was the best means to achieve his goals for personal freedom, self-determination, and human rights.

During the delivery trips, Parson observed and learned how cotton merchants managed most business transactions for Jacob. Henry and Parson delivered Jacob's cotton to the merchants, and they found the best place and time to sell it, earning a commission on the sale of the planter's cotton. The merchants also bought plantation supplies and sent them on to Jacob, taking another commission from these transactions. The relationship was remarkably informal, with few written contracts and legal disputes between Jacob and the merchants.

Parson learned about the cotton business in Southampton and memorialized it for his future use. Harvesting cotton on Jacob's farm gave him the opportunity to observe the intricate steps it takes to process cotton, starting with the planting of the crop to the point it becomes a specific consumer product. Parson envisioned that the cotton economy would return after the war. With a Union victory and the elimination of the enslavement codes, he could produce and market his own cotton crop.

Parson Met Frances and Chatted about the Call for Freedom

Near the Boykins Depot, Parson was happy to see and meet Frances Hill again. She instantly recognized him and walked boldly to the wagon, then looked him in the face. She smiled at him, and they fearlessly spoke to each other. Her eyes were dark and penetrating, without either fear or guilt. Her curly black hair waved wildly in the wind, as if resisting any form of restraint. Parson gathered from her fearless eyes, and her guiltless gestures that she was proud, with an unbroken independent spirit.

Long before speaking to her, Parson could tell she too desired natural human rights and craved freedom. Living both female and Black identities, Frances faced mistreatment from both racism and sexism. By living in Southampton, Parson knew the severe sexual exploitation of enslaved women, often bearing the children of their white masters or overseers. Enslaved women were defenseless against any type of abuse at the hands of white men. If an enslaved woman tried to defend herself, it would subject her to further beatings.

After the war, Jacob Williams' daughter, Parthenia Williams, stated she knew Frances Hill as a child. Frances went by the last name of Kindred, the family that owned her. As recalled by Parthenia, Frances may have had a brother who also went by the last name of Hill. Frances, much like other enslaved female, had no formal education. Frances' temperament complimented that of Parson. She did not accept without resistance the beliefs of the pro-slavery society in Southampton. Other than Frances' approximate birth year, about 1846, not much is known about her childhood and family background. Parthenia provided this information in the statement she gave with Frances' application for a veteran dependent pension.

Parson empathized and grieved with enslaved Black women. Sexual abuse of female slaves was endemic in the Southampton, where norms and customs treated all women as property or chattel. Sexual relations with enslaved women resulted in a notable increase of mixed-raced children born into slavery. The most common outcome of these forceful acts was the creation of a new child. The father might be her master, a neighboring white man, the overseer, or a slave assigned to her by her master. Slave laws did not recognize her marriage.

Parson felt comfortable with Frances. He revealed to her his urge to liberate himself by running away from Cross Keys, following an eastward path parallel to the railroad lines through Nansemond and Norfolk counties to reach the Union occupied city of Norfolk. His preparations followed the strategies and tactics for slavery resistance he learned about through the Black spoken network, as well as the moral justifications and motivation of the abolition movement. Parson told her about the discarded maps, pamphlets, and periodicals he found and their help in planning his self-liberation quest. He revealed to her where he guarded and kept in a secret location his collection of documents about freedom, abolitionists, resistance, and being reticent.

Frances revealed to him she played a small but vital role in the Underground Railroad and helped a few Southampton slaves escape to Norfolk and from there, they left to find sanctuary in Canada. Norfolk offered an urban environment for enslaved and freed Black people. Many of the enslaved Black people lived apart from their masters and could move freely throughout the town. According to Frances' comments, the Emanuel African Methodist Episcopal (A.M.E.) Church was a station house from which runaway slaves traveled north, and the attic was a lookout facility for the Underground Railroad.

The Black sanctuary community in Canada was an outcome of the conflict in the United States. After the British Empire abolished slavery in 1834, Canada became a major aim of Black people fleeing slavery in the United States. Fugitive slaves created a steady trickle of refugees into

Canada. These refugee communities received fugitive slaves throughout the eighteen-fifties and stayed closely tied to Black communities and abolitionists in nearby parts of the United States. Black Canadians received anti-slavery newspapers and listened to abolitionist lecturers from the U.S. When the Civil War broke out, they hoped it would end slavery and allow them to reunite with their families in the South. Black men from Canada enlisted in the United States Colored Troops regiments that had formed in 1863 and 1864.

Slave Culture and the Acculturation Process

As Parson developed a deeper understanding of the issues that sparked the Civil War, he pondered ways he could rise above and overcome the slave culture and the acculturation process. When Parson met Frances Hill, he recognized a need to bring to the consciousness of other enslaved men and women the unhealthy messages that they received through slavery and their effect upon Black male/female relationships. Enslaved men and women were chattel property. In many respects, the slave culture acculturation process was a means of survival and defiance against an inhumane ideology of racial superiority and inferiority. As opposed to a total slave rebellion, Southampton slaves practiced other forms of resistance. In these instances, slave culture significantly affected the economy and created a close-knit society with strong relationships between slaves.

The laws, culture, and principles of slavery that white people constructed were more sinister than racism; they created an oppressive, systematic way to dehumanize Black people. Frances did not consider herself to be an article of property without the ability to have feelings. She instinctively resisted enslavement because it was unnatural. As like Parson, she advocated and practiced a culture of resistance to survive and assert some measure of protest in an institution that treated people as property or things. Anecdotes memorialized Parson's reactions to and reflections on the effects of chattel slavery and provided a way to pass down to others in the family how he coped with chattel slavery hardships and resisted enslavement.

Parson and his brothers adopted a strong oral tradition, passing down anecdotes of a particular family incident or event, especially of an interesting nature. Because law proscribed slaves from reading or writing, oral tradition was a strong feature of slave culture and became the primary means of preserving slave history, mores, and cultural information, and this was consistent with the practices of oral history in Black cultures. Parson created anecdotes of Nat Turner to depict the struggles of Black on Jacob Williams' farm and memorialized his ways and means of liberation. He created a tale to assess current and desired status, another to explain the pursuit of self-liberation, and more tales that encouraged self-determination, self-development, and economic uplift.

Brigadier General Edward Wild's African Brigade

At family affairs, Parson proudly retold the story of Brigadier General Edward Wild's "African Brigade." He learned about his civilian-military tactics and military expeditions in Virginia and North Carolina from newspaper articles that covered the war. Brigadier General Wild was an adventurous and ardent abolitionist and a prime mover in the recruitment of Black men to Union military service. At the outbreak of the Civil War, he helped raise a company of the

First Massachusetts Infantry and fought at Bull Run and Fair Oaks before losing his left arm at South Mountain.

According to Parson, Brigadier General Edward Augustus Wild was an enthusiastic abolitionist and advocate in the recruitment of Black men to Union military service. At the outbreak of the Civil War, he helped raise a company of the First Massachusetts Infantry Regiment and fought at Bull Run and Fair Oaks before losing his left arm at South Mountain.

Inspired by the success of the 54th Massachusetts Infantry, the Governor John Andrew pushed for the creation of an entire brigade of United States Colored Troops. Brigadier General Wild took command of the first ever USCT brigade. He raised a unit of former slaves called Wild's African Brigade, which included the 55th Massachusetts Infantry, the 2nd North Carolina Colored Volunteers, and the 3rd North Carolina Colored Volunteers. He selected white officers to head the group of Black soldiers, and in April 1863, the African Brigade made its way to North Carolina to recruit local formerly enslaved Black men. White officers, it seemed, were not happy about serving with them, but the African Brigade performed courageously in battle.

In fulfilling his assignment to free slaves and gain recruits, General Wild freed over two-thousand five-hundred slaves, destroyed rebel camps, and executed the Confederate guerrilla, Daniel Bright. Wild not only recruited the newly freed Black people but then trained them and gave them the opportunity to prove their worth in battle.

On December 22, 1863, the Army organized the 2nd Regiment United States Colored Cavalry at Fort Monroe, Virginia and the 1st Regiment at Camp Hamilton, Virginia.

The regiments enrolled hundreds of former slaves from Suffolk, Nansemond, Isle of Wight, Great Bridge, and the rest of Hampton Roads were a reviled symbol of the mortal threat that Black men in blue Union uniforms posed to the status quo. Hampton Roads became a pioneering proving ground for the recruiting, training, and operational use of the newly formed United States Colored Troops. Eventually, the Army formed new regiments from every Union state.

While recruiting, General Wild liberated hundreds of slaves from plantations and resettled them on Roanoke Island. Next, they went to South Carolina to help in the capture of Charleston Harbor. The Brigade's remarkable success in the Carolinas displayed the efficiency of United States Colored Troops to the nation, fulfilling a crucial goal of Wild and his men. They continued to strengthen the reputation of Black troops in the eyes of the public.

During the winter of 1863, General Wild launched a major raid on Northeastern North Carolina. Designed to root out Confederate guerrillas and deprive southern sympathizers of their slave labor, Wild brought the heavy hand of war to coastal North Carolina. Although Confederate newspapers and officials labeled Wild as a "terror," the Union rewarded him with overall command of the Department of Norfolk on January 18, 1864.

USCT Regiments at the Battle of Fort Pocahontas

In 1864, the Union Army transferred General Wild's command to the Army of the Potomac, taking part in the Overland Campaign and the Siege of Petersburg. The African Brigade repulsed the Confederate troops at the Battle of Fort Pocahontas in the first pitched battle between Black troops and the Army of Northern Virginia.

As the war resumed, stories circulated about Black soldiers' participation in engagements and other crucial military service issues they faced. Because of prejudice against them, the Union did not use Black units combat initially. This was not the case with Brigadier General Wild. During the winter of 1863, he led these soldiers in an expedition on the coast of North Carolina, terrifying a local white population accustomed to Black slavery, the status quo since the era.

General Wild's USCT unit landed in Virginia in May 1864 at Wilson's Wharf on the James River in eastern Charles City, Virginia. By this time, the 10th USCT Regiment had a frightening reputation among Southerners. Wild's later actions alarmed them even more. His soldiers freed slaves and in one case whipped a plantation owner who had a reputation for harshness to his slaves. The presence of Black troops sent shock waves through Charles City County that rippled all the way to the Confederate capital thirty miles west. When word reached Southampton County of Black people bearing arms, it struck at the core of Jacob's fears, conjuring up images of Nat Turner's slave rebellion in 1831.

Soon, reports of atrocious outrages committed by General Wild's soldiers began appearing in Richmond newspapers. Wild helped fan the flames of Confederate anger, particularly when he allowed the public whipping of a civilian, William H. Clopton. According to Wild, Clopton was a very cruel slave master of notorious reputation who also was actively disloyal (Wild had rounded up several pro-Confederate civilians to prevent sabotage). When some of Clopton's female slaves showed Wild the scars they bore on their backs from whippings at their master's hands, a furious Wild turned the tables on Clopton. Wild ordered him stripped, and three of the slave women and one man took their revenge by whipping him by turns. When the Richmond newspapers reported the incident, however, the story transformed Clopton into three white men and the slaves into Wild's soldiers.

The Richmond papers denounced these activities and highly urged Confederate President Jefferson Davis to put a stop to General Wild's expeditions. Succumbing to the political pressure, Davis ordered Confederate Major General Fitzhugh Lee's cavalry division to break up this nest and stop their uncivilized proceedings. On May 24, elements of Fitzhugh Lee's cavalry division took a forty-mile march to reach Wilson's Wharf. The Confederate general expected a furious engagement at Fort Pocahontas with the Union defenders, but he found them alert and ready for action.

The two 10th USCT regiments under General Wild (about 1,800 men) repelled Fitzhugh Lee's cavalry division (about 3,000 men) attack on the Union supply depot at Wilson's Wharf. During the battle, also called the Battle of Wilson's Wharf, Brigadier General Edward A. Wild commanded 1,100 men and two cannons in a Union force that made up the 1st USCT Regiment and four companies of the 10th USCT Regiment. Battery M, 3rd New York Artillery, was the only all-white unit in the defenses. The gunboat USS Dawn lay in the James River to deliver fire support to the fort's defenders. The USCT soldiers were constructing a fortification there, later named Fort Pocahontas.

After Wild rejected Fitzhugh Lee's demand for a surrender, the Confederate cavalryman ordered his men to dismount and prepare for an assault. The 10th USCT soldiers in the fort repelled Fitzhugh Lee's soldiers in two separate rushes, during which only a handful of them reached the fort's ditch. When four more companies of the 10th USCT arrived by transport, Fitzhugh Lee called off further assaults.

General Wild's USCT unit killed or wounded about two hundred Confederate in the unsuccessful attack. Union losses were six killed and forty wounded. In his report, Fitzhugh Lee minimized both his strength and his losses. Southerners claimed that the action involved six gunboats and a substantial number of white Union soldiers. Ironically, it was the white soldiers who later committed attacks on civilian households: several of them broke into Sherwood Forest, destroyed furniture, stole family heirlooms, and tried unsuccessfully to bum the house. The engagement at Fort Pocahontas resulted in a Union victory by the Black garrison there and helped ensure the continued passage of Union vessels on the James River.

Parson and Francis Chatted Reactions and Reflected Freedom

Near the Boykins Depot, Parson was happy to see and meet Frances Hill again. Like Parson, she advocated and practiced a culture of resistance to survive and assert some measure of protest at an institution that treated people as property or things. They agreed that knowledge is a source of power, and she urged him to gain more knowledge with the warning to pretend to be ignorant of what Jacob commands of him. She amazed him and he admired she did not consider herself to be an article of property without the ability to have feelings. They enticed each other with romantic insinuations and passionate feelings but did not actually move on with each other.

Parson used his reactions to and reflections on freedom assessed the call for self-liberation. Before the Civil

War started, Parson discussed human rights and political implications of the abolition of slavery with his two brothers and a confidante, Henry Charity. They believed the Union fought the Civil War over the moral issue of slavery. Parson reacted to and reflected on the effects of chattel slavery and provided a way to pass down to others in the family how he coped with chattel slavery hardships and resisted enslavement. Since 1863, the Emancipation Proclamation both enraged the Confederacy with its promise of freedom for their slaves and threatened the very existence of its primary labor source. As the enlistment of free Black people and emancipated slaves grew, the Army organized the all-Black regiments.

To Jacob, it was the economics of slavery and political control of that system that was central to the war. The economy continued to suffer during 1864 as Union armies battered Confederate troops in nearby Petersburg. Before the war started, cotton plantations were very profitable, and Jacob got large tracts of land for little money. During the war, however, Union naval blockades hampered Jacob Williams' ability to sell cotton overseas. As Confederate territory dwindled under Union attack, invasion, and occupation, the traditional patterns of cotton cultivation and sales likewise came under assault. Newspaper articles and oral reports of Brigadier General Edward Wild's African Brigade haunted Jacob with reminiscences of the Nat Turner's Rebellion.

As he assessed the call for self-liberation, Parson's display of ignorance and illiteracy was a technique to help him repulse Jacob's oppression and the status quo.

Chapter Five
Broadsides, Brochures, and Newspapers

By early November 1864, much of the enslaved population of the Confederacy had found its way to freedom. As Black people walked off plantations and farms in vast numbers, many made their way to the Union controlled territories for food, clothing, and work. Before the Civil War, the anti-slavery press produced a steadily growing stream of newspapers, broadsides, brochures, speeches, abolitionist society reports, and memoirs of former slaves. During the war, broadsides, brochures, and newspapers were vital sources of information on the conflict, and as venues in which to attack and defend the issues that caused the Civil War.

The years of fighting took a devastating toll on the Confederacy's press. No sooner had the fighting started than newspapers and magazines in the eleven Confederate states experienced shortages of materials and staff that made publishing difficult, and, most times, impossible. As more areas of the Confederacy fell, Union troops wrecked or took over newspapers in the captured cities and towns. As the shortages and closings continued, less than half of the

Confederacy's newspapers and magazines were still publishing at the end of the war.

Going to the Boykins Depot gave Parson the opportunity to search through the depot waste for information and change his enslavement situation. He sought information on successful escapes of slaves from Southampton County who evaded the fugitive slave patrollers and crossed Union lines. What, he wondered nightly, would life be like after liberation from slavery and to be a Union soldier? Although the laws denied him freedom, Parson used a wide variety of strategies to contest Jacob's authority and to assert his human rights to control his own life.

Jacob Williams depended on involuntary labor to keep his farm solvent, but his enslaved workers often used work slowdowns to resist the theft of their labor. Continuous research and acts of resistance filled Parson's daily life on the Williams' farm. He revealed to Joseph and Henry information of Black men serving in the Virginia Peninsula as part of General Grant's Overland Campaign against Petersburg and Richmond. Black units were especially active in the fighting around Petersburg.

Parson Revealed His Vision of Self-Liberation

By November 1864, Parson had a clear vision of his plan to pursue self-liberation and enter the Union Army to fight for freedom. He revealed his vision and affirmed his intention of enlisting in the Union Army to his brothers. He called on them to confirm their commitment to join and contribute to the mission. If they fled Jacob's farm, he warned, they might fall into the hands of the home guard, private patrollers, confederate pickets, or fugitive slave hunters. After the brothers returned to their cabin each night, they secretly talked about different scenarios for their escape and liberation mission.

Parson told Joseph and Henry how he contemplated the mission to unfold and gave them detailed tasks, together with alternate scenarios, the suggested actions to take in response to obstacles, that he envisioned during the quest. Parson emphasized to both brothers that their aim was to achieve freedom from slavery and their specific goals were securing self-liberation, acquiring willful self-determination for themselves, and creating ways and means of uplift from their rock bottom economic conditions.

Each day when his work at the depot ended, Parson spent time in his secret haven. There, he secretly perused the discarded newspapers, magazines, and other documents to perform literature research on the mission on his own. Near a barely recognizable pig-path, hidden beneath Virginia Creeper vines, and fallen trees, he had about an hour per day in his haven to browse the scrounged documents for news about the war and his planned journey. Jacob and the members of his family were haunted by the raid on the haven during the Southampton Insurrection and were afraid to enter or come near it.

The Two Fugitive Slave Acts

The Fugitive Slave Law of 1793 allowed the return of fugitive-slaves to their owners and the Fugitive Slave Act of 1850 expanded the number of federal officials empowered to act in fugitive-slave cases. While in criminal cases public order was at stake, in fugitive-slave cases slave-owners stood to lose valuable property, making such situations both more legally complex and ripe for abuse. At the onset of the Civil War in 1861, Union troops in the field were unsure what to do with

Black people who escaped from slavery by crossing into Union lines. General Butler ordered that because Virginia had seceded from the Union, Jacob could no longer claim the protection of Fugitive Slave Laws. However, fugitive slave hunters from Union slave-holding states, like Delaware, remained a major obstacle in Parson's quest for freedom.

As ratified, the United States Constitution forbade free states from emancipating slaves who escaped from states where slavery was legal and mandated their return upon the claim of the slave-owner. It made state governments the primary actors when dealing with runaways. The state in which the capture of the runaway occurred had the obligation to deliver the slave to the state from which he or she had fled. By 1864, public opinion, at least among Union troops from antislavery hotbeds such as Massachusetts, had turned against such laws.

Parson discovered from reading broadsides, brochures, and newspapers that the United States Constitution still included a fugitive slave clause, which remained effective in slave-holding states that did not revolt and remained in the Union. Slave-owners in those states could claim their runaway slaves. Allegedly, some deceitful slave-owners tried to claim as fugitive slaves, Black escapees that they never owned. As told more than once, Parson considered the Fugitive Slave Laws as major obstacles to a successful quest for freedom. He knew this threat would remain until he was inside Union lines and confederate citizens could no longer claim the protection of United States laws.

Lincoln Declared the Emancipation Proclamation

When President Abraham Lincoln declared the Emancipation Proclamation, freeing all slaves in Confederate-controlled regions, the proclamation also allowed the enlistment of Black men in the Union Army. Parson was concerned about his physical fitness for enlistment in the Union Army. Henry Charity warned him about general physical characteristics that disqualified men for military duty covered a broad range of attributes that were more related to later development. The Union considered men too small, too sickly, or who had a sunken or narrow chest unfit for military service.

The proclamation enhanced Parson's thinking about possibilities for self-liberation and the call to action to escape from Southampton County to freedom. He thought more about what freedom meant and would bring into his life. He trusted that the Union Army understood the benefit and contribution of Black fighters and hoped the outcome would hasten the overthrow of the status quo by outlawing slavery.

As he came of age, he increasingly craved his freedom and to gain his liberty. Parson realized early in life that freedom was inherent and existed within him because of his humanity. To gain his liberty, he knew he must fight for the removal of the enslavement codes and laws that prohibited his enjoyment of freedoms, such as property rights, self-determination, and freedom of marriage.

Parson Studied Successful Slave Escapes

Since about mid-June 1864, Parson and his brothers listened anxiously to the roaring soundscape of artillery, cavalry and infantry forces clashing in and around Petersburg. Parson hoped the outcome of the nearby campaign would end victoriously for the Union forces and envisioned himself as a member of the winners. Through observation and examining his cache of printed material, Parson appreciated how the invention of the printing press delivered information to the masses, the invention of the telegraph created rapid communication; the railroad brought enhanced mobility, and how the development of economies of scale boosted wealth and power for the white men in the patriarchal Southampton society.

The invention of the printing press aided in the distribution of printed information of slave escapes to the masses. One of Parson's favorite studies of a successful slave escape was the story of Shadrach Minkins, the first escaped slave seized in New England under the 1850 Fugitive Slave Law. On February 15, 1851, slave catchers successfully apprehended Shadrach under the new law in Boston.

Born a slave in Norfolk, Virginia, Shadrach Minkins escaped to Boston in the spring of 1850 by stowing away on a ship bound for Boston harbor. There, he integrated into Boston's free Black community and supported himself by working as a server at the Cornhill Coffee House. Slave catchers, empowered by the Fugitive Slave Law, arrested Minkins with plans to return him to his owner in Virginia. On February 15, 1851, assistant deputy marshals took hold of Shadrach Minkins in the hallway outside the coffee room and took him to the courthouse, only a block away.

The sight of a fugitive slave being taken prisoner and herded toward the courthouse instantly became news, and within a short time Shadrach Minkins had a legal defense team and over one hundred supporters from Boston's Black community, to witness his hearing. While held at the courthouse, Minkins's supporters overwhelmed the federal officers, staged a daring rescue, and successfully escorted Minkins out of the city to safety in Canada.

From this story, Parson recognized the value of community support on his journey and realized the benefit of having a wise helper to aid and counsel him. For Parson, his father Solomon served this role and offered sage, sometimes hard-to-swallow advice.

Civil War Broadsides Informed the Citizens

Posted in public places, broadsides publicized and informed the citizens in Southampton County about current news events, official proclamations and government decisions, public meetings, and entertainment events, and more. Broadsides offered vivid insights into the daily activities and attitudes of individuals and communities that created America.

Broadsides advertised fairs and bazaars that women's groups held to raise money for their cause. Other publications advertised abolitionist rallies, some pictured in prints from contemporaneous periodicals. To build enthusiasm at their meetings, anti-slavery organizations used songs, some of which survived the war. They also used political and satirical prints from the eighteen-thirties through the eighteen-fifties that show the rising sectional controversy during that time.

Broadsides announced reward notices of various topics. In most cases, the reward notices were those seeking the return of runaway slaves. The reward notices gave a remarkably detailed description of fugitive slaves. Recruitment posters urged the men in Southampton County to support the Confederacy cause and enlist in military service. Older men, like Jacob who did not face conscription, who enlisted, received a bounty for their troubles, sometimes totaling several hundred dollars. This led to bounty jumping, in which the men would sign up, collect the cash, desert the army, and repeat the scheme.

Brochures Documented Slavery and Black Life

Brochures published during the Civil War provided Parson with information about political, social, religious, and intellectual issues of the day. There were many viewpoints presented in the brochures published by various organizations. They ranged from sermons discussing the morality of the war, to speeches by politicians expressing unique commentary on current events. Abolitionists and freed slaves circulated brochures that documented slavery and Black life in America. They had sermons, essays, reports, and other printed literature concerning attitudes toward slavery.

Brochures served as vehicles for northern Black people to protest. The slave narratives published as brochures by Black pamphleteers remained more independent of white editors than many slaves narrators. Their documents illuminated a much wider range of issues, from justifications of physically defending fugitive slaves to anti-discrimination efforts in northern communities.

Brochures were wonderful tools for discussions about the hopes and tactics of the Black abolitionists. Black people remained committed to the freedom struggle, and though their tactics may have changed, this commitment never wavered.

Newspapers in Virginia during the War

The war had a positive impact on the journalistic practices of the Union and Confederacy. Reporting methods and writing styles employed by the press changed to better cover the complexity and scale of the war. The standards for reporting and writing rose as editors set high expectations for their correspondents. They wanted war reporting stories that were truthful, complete, and prompt.

Newspapers in Virginia during the war contributed as vital sources of reporting on the conflict, and as venues in which to attack or defend the administration of Confederate President Jefferson Davis. At the start of the war, nearly every town in Virginia boasted a newspaper, with five dailies in Richmond alone. These papers were staunchly partisan: the Richmond Enquirer endorsed the Democratic Party, the Richmond Whig cheered on the Whig Party, and the Staunton Vindicator endorsed secession. During the war, they updated their readers on the Confederacy's military progress and relied on Northern papers when their own reporting failed.

Along with its rivals, the Enquirer announced victories and downplayed defeats, blurring the line between news and propaganda. The Richmond Examiner became the loudest voice of dissent in the Confederate capital. Its criticisms of President Davis turned more intense and personal as the war waged.

Rapid Communications Aided the Union's Victory

The telegraph found extensive use reporting breaking news. More than any other form of communication, the warring armies depended heavily on the telegraph. It was an important part of Civil War military and political history for two major reasons, as a tactical, operational, and strategic communication medium. For the first time in warfare, technology helped field commanders to direct real-time battlefield operations and allowed them to coordinate strategy across enormous distances. These capabilities were key factors in the Union's victory.

Another major reason was to keep civilian control over military and political activities. Because of civilian control of the telegraph, military commanders occasionally placed telegraph lines under martial law to ensure effective communication.

Mail via the Flag-of-Truce System

In August 1861, the United States banned the exchange of citizens' mail between the states in the Union and the Confederacy. Smugglers often carried mail illegally across the lines. The armies exchanged prisoner-of-war mail between the Union and Confederacy at designated points under a flag of truce. Citizens could also send letters via the flag-of-truce system, although like prisoners' mail, censors read their letters and rejected them if the contents were objectionable.

The Union Army assigned personnel to collect, distribute, and deliver soldiers' mail; wagons and tents served as traveling post office. Some soldiers wrote home weekly; some spent all their free time writing. Many soldiers carried letters in their pockets for delivery to loved ones on their behalf if killed in action.

In 1862, Fort Monroe served as a transfer point for mail exchange. The mail sent from states in the Confederacy addressed to locations in the Union sent by a flag-of-truce could only pass through Fort Monroe, where censors opened, inspected, resealed, marked and sent the mail on. Prisoner of war mail from Union soldiers in Confederate prisons also passed through this point for inspection.

In the 1864 election, twenty-five states would change their laws to allow soldiers to vote while away, either at a field station in their military encampment or by mail. The abrupt change in voting laws created a flurry in the 1864 election. Suddenly, soldiers with experience could comment on the candidates' war performances.

Major General Ambrose Burnside, Commander, Army of the Potomac

Major General Ambrose Everett Burnside was one of five generals to command the Union Army of the Potomac during the American Civil War. He received a Brevet Second Lieutenant position in the 2nd Artillery and served during the Mexican American War, mostly on garrison duty in Mexico City. After the war, he briefly served in garrison duty in the southwestern United States and resigned his commission in 1853. He set to work on a breech-loading rifle, which eventually failed, and later he rose to the rank of major general of the Rhode Island militia and received a nomination to Congress.

At the outbreak of the Civil War, General Burnside organized the 1st Rhode Island Infantry, which was one of the first units to arrive in Washington and offer the capitol protection. At the battle of First Manassas, Burnside commanded a brigade of infantry, and appointed brigadier general of volunteers on August 6, 1861, for his actions.

In September 1861, General Burnside took command of three brigades known as the Coast Division. His division successfully achieved a foothold in North Carolina, resulting in Burnside's promotion to major general in March 1862.

At the battle of Antietam, Union General George B. McClellan gave command of the Union Army IX Corps and

I Corps to General Burnside. During the Overland Campaign, General Burnside took part in the battles of the Wilderness, Spotsylvania Court House, North Anna, and Cold Harbor. General Burnside performed admirably in all the battles until the Battle of the Crater in Petersburg, Virginia.

USCT Soldiers at the Battle of the Crater

As reported in some newspapers, the United States Colored Troops figured prominently in the ill-fated Battle of the Crater fought on July 30, 1864, as part of the Petersburg Campaign. In utter confusion, Black and white Union units poured into a crater, which resulted from a planned mine explosion set off by Union soldiers under the small Confederate fort. The defending forces cut down the Union soldiers in the chaos, with Black people experiencing the heaviest single-day casualties of the war.

In 1864, the War Department reassigned the IX Corps to the Army of the Potomac. The largest concentration of Black soldiers on the Virginia Peninsula was the 4th Division of Major General Ambrose E. Burnside's IX Corps. At the end of April 1864, the 4th Division consisted of three brigades that included the 19th, 23rd, 27th, 30th, and 39th (USCT) Regiments; five companies of the 43rd Regiment; and four companies of the 30th Connecticut (Colored) Regiment. Other regiments were on the way to join it, from as far away as Illinois and Indiana. Its commander was Brigadier General Edward Ferrero, who had served with Burnside since the North Carolina Campaign.

According to historical military documents, on July 30, 1864, two weeks after the Union forces from Illinois and Indiana arrived outside of Petersburg, Virginia, the battle lines of both sides had settled into a stalemate. Union General

Ulysses S. Grant was reluctant to mount a frontal attack against well-fortified Confederate positions. By late June, Union forces controlled most of the eastern approaches to Petersburg. Neither side seemed ready to risk a major offensive move.

As the siege wore on, General Grant's men sought a way to break the stalemate. Colonel Henry Pleasants of the 48th Pennsylvania Volunteer Infantry Regiment, a mining engineer by profession, proposed to dig a mine running from the Union lines and under the closest Confederate fortification on the high ground within the Confederate line. Colonel Pleasants' proposal would excavate a large gallery, pack it with black powder, and then ignite the powder. This would make a vast hole in the enemy line, opening a path to Petersburg. Colonel Pleasants began digging on June 25, completing a 510-foot shaft within three weeks. By July 27, the mine packed with 8,000 pounds of gunpowder was ready to ignite.

At the end of July, General Grant approved the proposed explosion. Spearheading the Union attack was General Burnside's IX Corps. The Union plan was to exploit the explosion by sending the well-rehearsed 29th USCT Infantry Regiment of Edward Ferrero's 4th Division into the gap and driving for critical goals deep in the Confederate rear area. Burnside chose the 29th USCT Infantry Regiment assigned to Brigadier General Edward Ferrero's 4th Division, where all the ranks and file were Black to spearhead the assault.

The Union Army organized the 29th USCT Infantry Regiment at Quincy, Illinois, and mustered it into military service on April 24, 1864, three months before the Battle of the Crater. Though the 4th Division had spent most of their military service guarding army wagon trains and building fortifications, Burnside believed their enthusiasm and a chance to prove themselves in battle would compensate for their lack of combat experience. Burnside intended for Brigadier General Ferrero to give the 4th Division special training for the assault, but there is no evidence that he did so.

On July 26, General Burnside presented his attack plan to Major General George Meade. Believing that newly organized Black troops were unfit even for picket duty, General Meade refused to allow the 4th Division to lead the assault. However, he agreed to refer the question to General Grant, who was his superior. Meade convinced Grant by pointing out that if the Black troops led the attack and the Confederates massacred them, the public would believe that the Union Army cared nothing about Black soldiers. With the planned attack only twelve hours away on July 29, Grant ordered Burnside to select a white division to lead the assault on the crater instead of the 29th USCT Infantry Regiment, who he trained specifically for the task.

Despondent with the change in plans, General Burnside had his division commanders draw lots for the job and Brigadier General James H. Ledlie drew the lot to lead the attack. Ledlie's division was the smallest and weakest in the IX Corps, and since he did not brief his troops beforehand, they entered the crater out of curiosity instead of moving safely around its rim, as General Ferrero had trained the 4th Division to do.

The mine exploded at 4:44 a.m. on July 30, 1864. The results stunned everyone who witnessed it. When the dust settled, a crater 130 feet long, sixty feet wide and thirty feet deep scarred the landscape where the closest Confederate fortification had stood a moment before. The blast killed 352 Confederates. The Union, however, did not widen the breach. Instead, many Union soldiers plunged into the Crater. The Confederate defenders on either side of the Crater recovered quickly after their initial shock and poured fire from both flanks into General Burnside's men. Unable to exit the steep sides of the crater, the Confederates slaughtered them by firing down on General Ledlie's division. There were 3,798 Union troops casualties in the ill-fated battle that achieved none of its goals.

During the battle, Ledlie and Ferrero stayed behind the lines in a bunker, drinking liquor. Most damning for Ledlie's reputation was him not leading, or even going with, his men into battle, and a few weeks earlier, during the Battle at Cold Harbor, he had run and hidden for cover, an event that the soldiers did not forget, but which escaped Burnside's attention.

Eventually, the 29th USCT Infantry Regiment entered the fray, where it suffered heavy casualties. The Battle of the Crater was the first major action in which the regiment fought. The Crater was a debacle. General Grant relieved Burnside of command and had to find another way into Petersburg. He blamed Burnside and placed him on a leave of absence for the rest of the war. Several years after the Civil War's end, Grant apologized to General Burnside for blaming him for the debacle.

Parson Studied Information about Successful Slave Escapes

Working at the Boykins Depot gave Parson the opportunity to search through the depot waste containers for discarded, printed messages with actionable information from the cities and whistle stops along the Seaboard & Roanoke Railroad network. He also searched for non-military, political, economic, and social news reports, and articles about the abolition of slavery, and advertisement of successful slave escapes.

While moving around the depot, he discreetly glanced at the Confederate warmongering, secessionist, and pro-slavery broadsides and posters displayed around Boykins Town. He read and studied the announcements of events or proclamations, commentaries, or simply advertisements. He gave more attention to the information about fugitive slaves and their recapture by armed white men.

Parson studied news reports and articles about the abolition of slavery and advertisements of successful slave escapes. He learned that because Virginia had seceded from the Union, its citizens could no longer claim the protection of Fugitive Slave Law and Black people who escaped slavery by crossing into Union occupied territory were contraband. Parson read the scrounged newspapers and weekly magazine articles to gain knowledge about the Battle of the Crater and the 29th USCT Infantry Regiment operations.

Chapter Six
In Pursuit of Liberation and Equality

By November 1864, Parson was convinced that the Union Army understood the need for the abolishment of slavery, and he expected the Civil War outcome would end the status quo by outlawing the centuries-old institution. Countless acts of resistance marred everyday life on the Williams' farm. Although the law denied his freedom, Parson used a wide variety of strategies to contest Jacob's authority and to assert his rights to control his own destiny. Jacob depended on his involuntary labor to keep the family business solvent. Parson, Joseph, and Henry often used work slowdowns and malingering cleverly to gain some terms and conditions for their labor.

As the war surged on, many slaves ran east toward the Union forces but found little better treatment than they had as slaves. Food shortages became a severe problem in Southampton, and the slaves who stayed faced the same deprivations and hunger as their white women who took over the duties that their husbands had before the war. With so many slaves resisting and running away, Jacob feared another bloody uprising like the Nat Turner insurrection during which he had lost a wife, child, and a slave. He emphatically warned Parson, Joseph, Henry, and the other slaves on his farm that the unsympathetic Union government would work them harder than he ever did on government-owned cotton fields in Mississippi or Alabama to pay off the Union war debts.

Doubtful of Jacob's unfounded allegations, Louisa, his mother, feared the Confederacy would impress Parson and his brothers into their army, if instead they did not flee and enlist for Union military service. As the end of November 1864 drew near, Parson assured his mother that pursuing freedom, liberation, and equality meant everything to him. His decision to flee was final because liberation and equality are natural humanistic aspirations. He urgently resisted slavery and avoided helping the Confederacy cause in any manner. In Parson's mind, aborting his planned self-liberation quest was not an option. Enslavement ingrained in Parson's soul the will to cross the Blackwater River into Union controlled Nansemond County in pursuit of liberation and equality, and the urge to uplift himself from his rock bottom economic conditions.

Parson had an absolute obsession with his work at the Boykins Depot, and the opportunities to search for news about the war and articles related to the abolition of slavery. In particular, he looked for posted notices of successful slavery escapes and advertisements for their capture and return. He read newspapers and weekly magazine articles to gain knowledge about military service and the army's engagements. After sunset and darkness ended his daily work, Parson escaped from the farm and meandered into the thick forest to his haven. The blood of the Southampton Insurrection victims still stained the floors inside the alleged old, abandoned Francis' house, and no member of the Williams family would ever enter his haven.

Harvesting Peanuts on Rachael Worrell Tract

On Jacob's farm, Louisa prepared the morning meals at daybreak. When Parson arose, there was a smell of breakfast on the table, the same as was there every day, and he would not have it any other way. Roasted peanuts upon the stovetop, his favorite snack. Louisa prepared the breakfast of salted slab pork, a whole fruit, lots of cheese, gravy covered biscuits, and coffee substitute made from peanuts.

According to historical writings, the popularity of peanuts surged during the Civil War when soldiers recognized and depended upon peanuts as a food source. The peanut made its way to Virginia on sailing ships that imported slaves before this practice ended in the United States. Although there were some commercial peanut farms before the Civil War, Jacob did not grow peanuts extensively. He lacked interest in peanut farming because the growing and harvesting techniques were slow and difficult, along with the fact that he regarded the peanut as food for the enslaved and poor people.

Caswell Worrell grew peanuts under his uncle's management and started harvesting the crop in late October through the end of November. Parson and the younger slaves were not exempt from work growing and harvesting peanuts. During harvesting season, Jacob assigned Caswell to oversee work on the peanut crop. The Sykes brothers planted peanuts on the farm in the early spring and harvested the crop in the fall. If planted in early spring, the leaves on the peanut plant fell from the vines in the fall, the brothers plowed and dug the crop. When fully matured, the plant dropped its leaves, and after the leaves fell off, the vines were of very little value as hay. However, Jacob considered the vine excellent animal fodder and tried to harvest the crop in time to secure good hay.

To harvest the crop, the brothers used a mule-powered plow to dig up the peanuts so that the loosened vines would not have soil thrown upon them. Next, they plowed space along both sides of the rows, just near enough for the plow wing to reach the taproot. Finally, with pitchforks, they lifted the vines from the loose soil, shook them to remove the soil, and then laid them down, either singly or in small piles, to wilt and cure in the sun.

During the War, Caswell and Jacob sold the peanuts to brokers who shelled, cleaned, and graded the raw nuts before selling them to companies. Later, in the eighteen-nineties, Parson met Benjamin Hicks, a Black farmer from Southampton County, who invented a gasoline-powered machine for digging up and cleaning peanuts. He received a patent for the device but faced a lawsuit from the most powerful farm-equipment companies of the time. Hicks won in court in 1901, and his invention helped modernize peanut farming. Years later, Parson's grandsons grew peanuts commercially and ran a brokerage firm.

Seaboard and Roanoke Railroad Connections

Parson found a discarded 1847 map of the Seaboard & Roanoke Railroad showing the railroad connections from Southampton to Norfolk Counties, Virginia. The railroad connections extended from the Boykins Depot to Portsmouth, Virginia. After studying the map. Parson presumed that following along the railroad connections route from Boykins to Norfolk County was a plausible escape route to reach Fort Monroe.

According to Official Records of the Civil War, the Confederate government did not consider the Seaboard & Roanoke Railroad as very important during the Civil War, especially when they had to abandon Norfolk County in 1862. The government in Richmond ordered the railroad's iron stripped and used for the construction of an extension to the Roanoke Valley Railroad. The Confederate government ordered the rolling stock transferred and leased to other more important railroads. During the siege of Suffolk, there was an effort made to remove the iron from the Seaboard & Roanoke Railroad. Beginning near Suffolk, the Confederate engineer department removed about three miles of the rails and removed it toward Franklin and deposited it at or near a place known as Beaver Dam.

From the runaway slave notices posted in the depot, Parson recognized that slave-patrollers collected information about the runaways' routes, destinations, and motives. As tacitly described in their advertisements, slaveholders knew that Southampton's self-liberating men and women drew on kinship bonds and a sophisticated familiarity of the surrounding counties to plan their escape routes and final destinations. While Jacob expected Parson, Joseph and Henry would decide to pursue self-liberation, he had at his disposal an elaborate network of surveillance to chase, capture, and reclaim escaped slaves.

Potential Routes and Final Destination of the Runaways

In their escape attempts, Southampton enslaved people showed their awareness of the surrounding military, legal, and political situations. Parson sought information from Solomon, Louisa, and family acquaintances. He thought he might have to rely on trustworthy people in nearby areas to aid them at the designated points along the journey. He revealed to Solomon the potential routes he was considering and the plausible destinations to gain his advice and counsel. Parson listened to Solomon's advice and description of refugee camps in Hampton and Craney Island.

According to Solomon, when the war began, the confederate forces guarded the Blunts Bridge, crossing over the Blackwater River as a part of the Blackwater defensive line. But in November 1862, the invading Union forces drove the Confederates away from the bridge and captured their supplies but left the bridge standing. The Union forces fought another skirmish on March 9, 1863, that resulted in the same outcome. The Confederate forces set up and kept a defensive line along the west banks of the Blackwater River for the duration of the war.

Solomon informed Parson that the Union Army categorized freed slaves who arrived at Fort Monroe as contraband of war. They lived as refugees in small huts in Hampton, Virginia, employed as military laborers, and survived off food from the military and donations from Northern sympathizers. Other freed slaves were living in a refugee camp on Craney Island, in Norfolk County. The 10th Infantry Regiment USCT occupied the small island after the Union recruited and armed Black soldiers in Hampton Roads. In May 1864, the regiment joined

General Butler's operations on the south side of James River and against Petersburg and Richmond.

Parson told Solomon and Louisa about Frances and the desire to marry her one day and live together in a household. Parson constantly envisioned a wife and family in his future. Frances was the perfect match for Parson. She was more than a beautiful young woman; she was a woman whose inner beauty was externally recognizable. Frances displayed her spirit in her actions and in her appearance. Like Parson, Frances resisted enslavement too and defied the status quo. In reaction to slavery, she malingered, feigned illness, and destroyed property to undermine the confederacy victory.

The Risks of Fleeing Slavery

In Southampton County, slave culture was the reactions and resistance to racial inequality and social injustice. Parson held the belief that a proactive form of resistance was necessary to gain political, economic, moral change and rid the society of inequality. Self-liberation did not rely on passive responses to slavery and exploitation of Black people. Instead, it presented an avenue for like-minded individuals to take control and gain their freedom.

Parson resisted his enslavement by fleeing and leaving it. Fleeing slavery was dangerous, but enslaved people successfully fled Southampton to freedom. Parson knew he and his brothers would need to implement counter-tracking measures to evade the elaborate network of surveillance, chase, and capture during the flight. It was important for them to avoid slave patrols, local law officers, suspicious farmers, hostile dogs, even bloodhounds, by not traveling on a known route or calling attention to themselves.

According to oral family history recounted many times, Parson and his brothers understood and used different measures allegedly practiced by Nat Turner to evade patrollers. He used different measures to cover his tracks and help make a longer hideaway. The different measures included leaving no trace, staying out of sight, and using deception.

People said Nat Turner knew what not to leave behind to avoid tipping off the tracker to your trail. He avoided soft, impressionable areas of ground that readily capture tracks because they would leave so much information behind. As he passed by low-hanging tree limbs, he tried not to bend or break them. He tried to travel when the wind was blowing so it would blow away his tracks. He knew that walking in a wooded area with lots of leaves or pine needles on the ground, he would not leave much in terms of footprints, and he was careful not to leave behind evidence as snapped twigs and overturned leaves.

While on the run, Nat Turner stayed out of sight and moved when visibility was low, such as nighttime, stormy weather, or snowstorms. He knew how to use your surroundings as a natural disguise. To avoid silhouetting, he stayed off ridges and the tops of hills. When moving, he kept low to the ground, making sure nothing was in his background besides the sky.

To evade his pursuers, Nat Turner implemented some deception tactics to throw chasers off his trail. The chasers looked for which direction gravel and dirt he dragged in relation to the print. When he walked backward, he dragged the dirt in the direction he walked, not the direction he wanted to make them think he traveled. He also doubled back when he walked and left a trail in a general direction but then walked backward over his tracks to a jump-off point. Nat Turner's trackers followed his initial line of tracks and bypassed his jump-off point.

Parson and his brothers discussed, rehearsed, and practiced how to use the different evasive measures Southampton enslaved people alleged Nat Turner practiced evading patrollers.

Enrollment Act (The Conscription Act)

To the Sykes brothers' delight, the United States Army began actively recruiting Black men for military service in September 1862, after President Abraham Lincoln issued his Preliminary Emancipation

Proclamation. The Enrollment Act changed everything. An amendment to the act that had instituted conscription one year earlier, it specified that male slaves, even those of loyal masters, for the first time became eligible for the draft. Federal agents established a quota of new troops for each congressional district.

Applauded by abolitionists, the document troubled some Northerners who initially supported the war as a necessary means to preserving the Union. Driven by racism and fears of competing for scarce jobs with potential waves of formerly enslaved Black people immigrating from the south, many northern workers lost what little enthusiasm remained for volunteering to fight in a prolonged crusade for freeing southern slaves. A subsequent decline in enlistments prompted the government to abandon the unwieldy and ineffective state-administered drafts with a new mechanism for implementing compulsory military service on a national scale.

The Enrollment Act declared that all able-bodied male citizens of the United States, and persons of foreign birth who shall have declared on oath their intention to become citizens between the ages of twenty and forty-five years were declared to make up the national forces and shall be liable to perform military duty in the service of the United States when called out by the President for that purpose. The act made it lawful for the executive of the states to send recruiting agents into any of the states declared to be in rebellion, except the states of Arkansas, Tennessee, and Louisiana, to recruit volunteers.

Three provisions of the act were so unpopular that they spawned protests, riots, racially motivated violence, and the assassinations of draft officials in several states. Those items stated any person drafted and notified to appear may furnish an acceptable substitute to take his place in the draft. Next, any person eligible for the draft could pay the government a commutation fee not greater than $300 to receive an exemption. The act allowed free Black citizens to volunteer for service but exempt from the draft. Effectively, any person drafted had ten days to hire an acceptable substitute, pay a $300 commutation fee, or report for service. Failure to do so would lead to prosecution.

The urban poor found these provisions particularly objectionable because of the economic discrimination against them. That affluent Americans who could readily afford to hire substitutes or pay a commutation fee of $300 to avoid service led to the adoption of the slogan rich man's war, poor man's fight. The sum of $300 was roughly equivalent to the annual wage of unskilled workers in the day; thus, the funds needed to hire a substitute or pay the commutation fee were beyond the reach of most urban dwellers. In contrast, prominent white men could take advantage of the exemptions to hire substitutes or become $300 men. According to published reports, Grover Cleveland, twenty-six at the time of his enrollment in June 1863, paid George Beniski, a thirty-two-year-old Polish immigrant, to serve in his place as a private in the Seventy-sixth New York Infantry.

Urban White men opposed the Enrollment Act because of the possibility of being forced to do so, while it exempted free Black men from the draft. Racism, combined with concerns about formerly enslaved people migrating north after the war to compete for jobs and potentially driving down wages, made urban whites less than enthusiastic about joining a war to free southern slaves.

Implementation of the Enrollment Act provoked violence and invited evasion. In New York City, two days after the first draft lottery on July 11, 1863, an angry mob, consisting mostly of Irish immigrants, attacked and burned the assistant provost marshal's office in the Ninth District, sparking four days of rioting. Besides violence, the Enrollment Act also evoked evasive tactics. Men with the means to do so, illegally bribed doctors for medical exemptions. Labor unions, employers, political parties, draft insurance societies, and even local governments raised funds to pay the $300 cost for individuals to avoid the draft.

The evasive tactics and violence spawned by the Enrollment Act prompted Congress to amend the legislation twice. An 1864 revision limited the term of the $300 exemption to one year, after which draftees had to serve. That revision resulted in the prevailing rates for substitutes to balloon. A second change in 1865, designed to reduce the number of dissenters crossing the border into Canada, imposed the loss of citizenship on draft dodgers and deserters.

Astonishingly, there was remarkable compliance with the Enrollment Acts. The participation of a million white soldiers and 180,000 Black soldiers in the war depicted the lack of resistance to the draft legislation. While bounties were expensive, they resulted in an all-volunteer Union Army during the war. The Enrollment Act was a national law enforced locally, and the resistance to the law revealed the legal and popular opposition to a federal draft act. But it revealed the racism within urban communities that the conscription legislation brought to the surface.

Major General George Meade, Commander, Army of the Potomac

In June 1863, General George Meade became the commander of the Army of the Potomac. He defeated Robert E. Lee and the Army of Northern Virginia in the Battle of Gettysburg (1863) and led the major Union army in Virginia until the end of the war. George G. Meade was a Union major general and one of the most important commanders of the Civil War.

The Army of the Potomac was in turmoil. Lincoln had long bemoaned George B. McClellan's lack of aggressiveness in the Virginia campaigns of 1862. When McClellan could achieve only a limited victory over Lee's army at Antietam and did not undertake active operations immediately after the battle, replaced him. First Lincoln replaced him with Major General Ambrose E. Burnside, who led the army to a stunning defeat at Fredericksburg, and then by Major General Joseph

Hooker, who lost at Chancellorsville although his forces outnumbered those of the Confederates.

President Lincoln promoted Ulysses S. Grant to the command of all the Union armies in February 1864. Grant avoided having his headquarters in Washington; instead, he would go with Meade's army and allow Meade to command his troops while the new general-in-chief would coordinate all the Union spring offensives. Grant informed Meade that his aim was Lee's army—wherever it went, the Army of the Potomac would go.

Grant increasingly dictated tactical orders for Meade to conduct. In addition, some of Grant's staff officers looked down on Eastern soldiers and felt that he should remove Meade from command. Grant saw Meade was a capable army commander and said so often. He received most of the blame for the army's high casualty rate during the fighting.

During the siege operations, Grant instructed Meade when to launch offensives aimed at extending the Union siege lines and wearing down Lee's army. Meade's well-known irascibility manifested itself more and more than the operations, and he could not prod his corps commanders into decisive attacks. When General Burnside was ready to explode his mine under the enemy earthworks, General Meade vetoed Burnside's plan to use a division of Black troops because he feared an abolitionist backlash if these soldiers failed to live up to expectations. During the fighting on July 30, 1864, at "the Crater" left by the mine explosion, Burnside and Meade got into a heated argument after Meade accused his corps commander of sending misleading reports about the battle.

Meade led the army from the Wilderness to Spotsylvania, the North Anna River, and across the James River to assault Petersburg in mid-June. By that time, the Army of the Potomac had suffered at least 50,000 casualties, including many experienced regimental, brigade, and division commanders. By the time the Petersburg operations began, the army was much less responsive than it had been when the campaign started in May. As a result, a frustrated Meade could not prod his subordinates to launch coordinated attacks. Both warring sides constructed earthwork forts and entrenched, and a stalemate existed until April 1865.

29th Infantry Regiment, USCT in Battle of Weldon Railroad

On May 4, 1864, Grant launched his Overland Campaign when the Army of the Potomac crossed the Rappahannock and Rapidan Rivers, occupying an area locally known as the Wilderness. In the meantime, the 29th United States Colored Infantry Regiment took part in the Battle of Weldon Railroad. The Union Army mustered the 29th Infantry Regiment, USCT into military service on 24 April 1864 and attached to the 2nd Brigade, 4th Division, IX Corps, Army of the Potomac where all the ranks and files were Black. The 29th Infantry, USCT Regiment guarded the army wagon train and dug trenches for a few weeks.

General Grant launched his fifth offensive on August 18, 1864, with orders to destroy a section of the railroad and hold it. Grant believed that isolating Petersburg was the only way to win the campaign. It forced the Confederates to carry their supplies thirty miles by wagon to bypass the new Union lines extended farther to the south and west. The Battle of Weldon Railroad was the first Union victory of Grant's Overland Campaign.

Major General Gouverneur K. Warren's V Army Corps and elements of the IX and II Corps reached the Weldon Railroad on August 18 and withstood a counterattack about three-quarters of a mile north of the tracks that afternoon. The first troops to reach the tracks arrived around 9:00 a.m. The Union soldiers slowly moved northward, leaving heated rails twisted in the shape of the V Corps' insignia.

In pouring rain, the Union soldiers scattered the confederate gunners and deployed across the tracks near a small house. Between 2:00 and 3:00 p.m., gunfire erupted in the thick woods as three Confederate brigades led by General Henry Heth pounded southward against Warren's men. The confederates drove the Union soldiers south about three-quarters of a mile, while Warren frantically called up reinforcements and artillery support. Heth withdrew to a line parallel to our location after the engagement turned into a static fire fight.

The first day of the Battle of Weldon Railroad ended with 1,000 Union casualties and about 350 for Heth. The Union soldiers still held the tracks, but the stage was now set for a more powerful Confederate attack the next day.

The next day, Confederate General William Mahone sliced between Warren's right flank and the IX Corps' left, inflicting a tactical defeat on the Union, including the loss of over 2,500 prisoners. The prompt arrival of reinforcements, however, kept the Union forces in place across the critical rails. Two days later, Mahone struck again, this time aiming for Warren's left flank, beyond the alignment of the railroad to the west. Mahone acted, however, on inaccurate information. Instead of striking the flank and rear of the Union position, his assault hit the Union soldiers head-on, with predictable results. Some sixty percent of his men fell under withering fire.

On August 19, General Mahone attacked with five infantry brigades, rolling up the right flank of Union forces. General Warren counterattacked and by nightfall had retaken most of the ground, lost during the afternoon's fighting.

On August 20th, the Union laid out and entrenched a strong defensive line covering and extending east to connect with the main Union lines. On August 21, General A. P. Hill probed the new Union line for weaknesses but could not penetrate the Union defenses. The three days of fighting along the Weldon Railroad cost the Union Army 4,279 casualties.

Parson Resolved to Escape Bondage in Southampton County

In Southampton County, slave culture was the reactions and resistance to racial inequality and social injustice. Parson held the belief that proactive forms of resistance would gain political, economic, social change and rid the American society of inequality. Parson now believed that the war was over the moral issue and economics of slavery. Like many enslaved Black people in the county, Parson opts to flee enslavement, although escape attempts were dangerous and uncertain.

After studying the map. Parson presumed that following along the railroad connections route from Boykins to Norfolk County was a plausible escape route to reach Fort Monroe. He understood the challenges from the Confederate pickets who patrolled west of the Blackwater and border states enforced the Fugitive Slave Acts east of the river. Still, thousands of enslaved Black people successfully fled in pursuit of freedom and human equality.

By 1864, widespread opposition to the Fugitive Slave Act of 1850 made the law unenforceable in Northern states, and by 1860, Slave Hunters successfully returned only a few enslaved people to their slaveholders. Representatives in congress regularly introduced bills and resolutions to repeal the Fugitive Slave Act, but the law persisted until June 28, 1864, when Congress repealed both acts.

In the meantime, the Enrollment Act of February 24, 1864, changed everything. The act specified that Black male slaves, even those of loyal masters, for the first time became eligible for enrollment.

Chapter Seven
Parson Revealed Escape Plan

Since the Nat Turner insurrection in 1831, Southampton slave owners dreaded another large rebellion, especially one where a self-liberated Black man was leading the revolt. Self-liberation would add many angry formerly enslaved people to the USCT ranks and files of those who wanted to emancipate the remaining enslaved people violently. Regardless of how horrendous life as a slave proved to be in Southampton County, it was no simple decision to run away. Escaping involved leaving behind parents, love interest, and heading into an unknown territory, enduring harsh weather, a river to cross, and the constant threat of capture by Confederate sympathizers, cavalry pickets, bands of guerrillas, and fugitive slave catchers from Union border states.

For Parson, self-liberation involved the actions of an enslaved person freeing him or herself from the bondage of slavery. If allowed, the easiest way of self-liberation was for an enslaved person to pay the slaveholder for freedom, which many tradespeople and urban slaves did. There are several other stories of the various ways to escape enslavement, but the most extreme way to end bondage was by death. Living near Union armies, Parson took advantage of the opportunity to run to freedom, and as the likelihood of groups escaping together increased over the course of the war. The Union Army's occupation of Suffolk left the Blackwater River as the demarcation line between Union and Confederate controlled territory. Living in Southampton County on Jacob's farm, Parson could flee toward Franklin and be safely within Union lines after only a six hours' journey.

On December 1, 1864, Parson completed his escape plan, collected and stored provisions, gathered carpentry tools for weapons, grabbed Seaboard & Roanoke Railroad map and other equipment needed during his journey. Alone in his haven, he drew strength from his convictions that liberation and equality were good things, realizing that he must seek freedom for its own sake. His only regret was that he might not see Francis again. While Francis did not escape with him, she served a critical role in helping Parson to see himself as a man of unbounded independence, with an ultimate vision to liberate himself and his companions.

Parson Conceived His Escape Plan

Occasionally at Boykins Depot, Parson watched the men in the county home guard unit assemble to receive their daily assignments and get updates on the course of the war from their sergeants. The home guard included local men over the age of forty-five and under eighteen. The guard's duties were arresting deserters, patrolling slaves, policing residents suspected of having pro-Union sympathies and protecting supplies for the army. In Parson's view, as he conceived his escape plan, Jacob's first line of defense against his self-liberation was considered the home guard.

The details of Parson's escape plan changed as he developed it, but when he met and proposed his improved plan to his brothers Joseph and Henry, they were enthusiastic but doubtful. In a manner like the home guard sergeants, he told them about the plausible travel route east toward Norfolk on foot under protecting darkness and then sail on a steamer to Fort Monroe. He showed them the railroad map and pointed out areas of special interest to avoid or to seek help. He recommended the brothers accumulate a few items they might need to complete the estimated day and a half trip to freedom.

Joseph and Henry agreed, if Parson were right, then his proposal to reach Fort Monroe would give them freedom and a chance to enlist in the Union Army. But they cautioned him that racism has existed in the United States since the colonial era and still probably would exist after their liberation. Parson acknowledged that but liberation and equality, he pleaded, is everything and he does not care about the pain and suffering that would come to him while pursuing his commitment to self-liberation and emancipation. They knew if slavery remained legal anywhere in the United States, the fugitive slave patrol would have to follow the warrants seeking the return of runaways, which he reassured them that the Union Army would resist. To ease their doubt, Parson assured them that the Union Army would not enforce warrants from the confederacy seeking the return of fugitive slaves.

After he explained the concept of his escape plan to his enslaved brothers and urged them to join him, they were more enthusiastic. The Union Army occupied Nansemond County from the left bank of the Blackwater River, around Suffolk City, and the territory throughout Norfolk County. Their conclusion was unanimous: self-liberation and equality are good things. They must resist slavery and rejection of the escape proposal was not an option.

Parson Completed His Escape Plan

Parson worked ferociously on his escape plan, collecting, and storing provisions in his haven, gathering small tools for weapons, securing his railroad line connections map and other apparatus to employ it for the good of society. He developed a plan to minimize the effects of contact, connection, or communication with the populace. Parson focused his escape plan on the mission, tasks, and activities that supported the goal and prevented capture by Confederate pickets, their sympathizers, bands of guerrillas, and fugitive slave catchers. Parson included suggested ways to avoid areas that would risk becoming recruited for confederate military service or impressment back into enslavement.

Around noon on December 2, 1864, Joseph and Henry stole away from their work at the Worrell farm to look for Parson. They knew from childhood where he sought haven after working at the depot. Parson was happy to see them and hoped that they were ready to join his quest for freedom. Convinced the proposed plan would work, they agreed to join him later that evening, under cover of darkness, after completing their peanut harvesting tasks routinely, to avoid giving Caswell any hint of the plan.

According to oral portrayals, enslaved Southampton people sought various methods of liberation everywhere they could, even in modes as specific as their choice of clothes. They used several means to escape slavery and were always the initiators of their own liberty. Just like Nat Turner, they did not wait around for proclamations and decrees. Slave catchers captured most slaves who escaped from bondage in Southampton and returned them to their owners and endured severe punishment. Despite the dangers, however, many runaways found their way north to places that outlawed slavery.

Parson Revealed the Escape Plan

Later, on December 2, 1864, Parson secretly gathered his trusted cohorts at his haven to deliver the final escape plan. When Joseph and Henry arrived and gathered in the haven, Parson revealed to them the mission, goals, aim and detailed the tasks to execute the plan. As Parson said, the mission of their self-liberation quest is to cross into Union controlled Nansemond County, navigate to and reach Union controlled and occupied Norfolk, enlist and successfully complete military service, and return to Southampton to live freed and liberated.

Parson realized and reflected on the hardship, danger, and difficulty of escaping from slavery. He knew it would be difficult because of the incredible physical challenge of the forty-three-mile journey to freedom. Most runaways were young men like Joseph, twenty-six-years old; and Henry, about twenty-three-years old, who were practically illiterate, and had little money and few possessions. The color of their skin made them easy targets during the daylight for racist patrollers and fugitive slave catchers. Mindful of this, Parson assigned Joseph and Henry appropriate roles and responsibilities.

While the escape plan took advantage of the opportunity to run to freedom across the nearby Blackwater River, Parson did not take into consideration the possibility of the Sykes family escaping together. This was a critical weakness and drawback in the escape plan Parson revealed. The fear of separation through the sale of one or more family members always haunted Solomon and Louisa, who knew how likely it was to happen. Even though Jacob once remarked that having enslaved families together made it much less likely that a man or woman would run away, but these remarks from him were no comfort to Louisa. Solomon told his family that slavery was immoral on many grounds, and the separation of a family during self-liberation was one of them. Solomon and his sons pledged to find all family members when slavery and the war were over, and to bring the Sykes family back together.

The escape plan involved and covered the movement of the brothers through contested conditions from Jacob's Williams farm in Boykins to Union controlled and occupied Norfolk. Parson based and planned the eastward escape route with caution and the anticipation of the constant threat of capture by slave patrollers, either en route or shortly after arrival at the destination. Once executed, the escape movement ended if captured or when the cohorts reached Norfolk. Because the escape plan movement shares many of the characteristics of hide and seek, an old children's game, Parson organized the escape plan path of travel in segments like hide-and-seek rounds.

Parson, who began the self-liberation plot, emerged as the established leader of the journey. Joseph and Henry recognized his strong communications skills, his clear vision of the escape plan's end-result, and his ability to motivate them. As the leader, he realized how important it was to know his location during the entire movement. Without constant awareness of their location, the cohorts cannot expect to conduct the mission. To ensure the correct location, Parson named Joseph as navigator and Henry as the pacer.

Joseph helped with navigation by ensuring that the brothers always remained on the plan course. Parson thoroughly briefed him on the first path parallel to the Seaboard & Roanoke Railroad and supplied subsequent instructions as necessary on the segments. Henry, the pacer, always kept the pace of travel. Parson chose how often Henry set and reported the pace at the end of each segment of the journey.

From living and traveling throughout the forests and swamps in Southampton County, Parson understood how to navigate in the terrain based on methods allegedly practiced by Nat Turner. Parson used the moon, stars, and sun to figure out his location and direction, to stay on the right path, and to tell the time of day. According to folklore, Nat Turner would look in the sky to see where the sun was, and from its position, he knew where to find the north. Likewise, Parson knew the sun always rose in the east and set in the west, as well as where to find the north.

On nights in which he could see the moon, Parson used it to navigate just like he used the sun. He knew moonlight was the reflection of sunlight on the moon's surface and its shadow was in a directional relationship to the sun's position. He knew when he faced the full moon, and the sun was right behind him. Parson observed when the moon was new and saw its thin crescent. He knew that the sun was in front of him, under the horizon.

Folks said Nat Turner used stars to figure out how to set out on the right path. He knew that the North Star in the night sky always pointed North. He also knew how to pick it out from all the other stars because he knew it was based around the Big Dipper, one of the most easily identifiable star patterns in the night sky.

Folks also said Nat Turner used trees, moss, ants, and plants to find the direction if other methods did not work. He knew trees grew their branches in the direction that receives the most sun, facing south side. Moss grew on any hard surface, including the sides of trees, but it grew on north-facing surfaces because it liked the darker, more humid environment. If Nat Turner did not see any moss growing on trees, he checked for moss on rocks. After he checked for moss, he looked around the base of some trees for ants. Ants built their colonies exposed to the most sunlight, which was normally facing south. Plants faced south to receive the most sunlight which was necessary for their growth. Nat Turner knew a patch of thick, luscious vegetation in the forest was probably facing on a southward slope.

After Parson delivered his escape plan, assigned duties, and rehearsed navigation methods, Joseph and Henry returned to the Worrell farm and completed their daily work. Parson recommended they prepare for departure on a minute notice and get some rest. The brothers collected and packed a few pounds of peanuts, plugs of tobacco, some of Jacob's winter clothes, and bedding to employ during their journey. While planning and preparing, Parson analyzed the railroad map and marked out a route that helped navigation, gave advantage to friendly areas, and probable locations of adversaries. In addition, he looked at the map to decide areas or features that could aid navigation, become possible intermediate segments, and used for bivouac areas.

Major General Charles Jackson Paine

Among the most astute political generals of the war was Major General Charles Jackson Paine. He graduated from Harvard in 1853 and in 1861 he entered the Federal service as a captain in the 22nd Massachusetts Infantry and as a colonel of the 2nd Louisiana Infantry. Parson learned of his military and civilian background from discarded newspapers and occasionally retold his story at family gatherings.

Major General Charles Jackson Paine was an American railroad executive, soldier, and yachtsman who was commanding general of the Third Division of the XVIII Corps in the Union Army during the Petersburg Campaign. In 1861, he entered the Federal service as a captain in the 22nd Massachusetts Infantry.

The great-grandson of Robert Treat Paine, a signer of the Declaration of Independence, General Paine was born August 26, 1833, in Boston. In September 1861, he recruited a company of the 22nd Massachusetts Infantry, and he entered service with them as a captain on October 5, 1861. The next year, the Army sent him to Ship Island, Mississippi. In October, he became the first colonel of the 2nd Louisiana Infantry. During the siege of Port Hudson, from May 24 to July 8, 1863, he commanded a brigade.

On March 8, 1864, Paine resigned his colonel's commission to accept a position on the staff of General Benjamin F. Butler, who secured his appointment as brigadier general of volunteers on July 4, 1864. Paine took part in the attack on Drewry's Bluff; commanded a Black division at New Market in September; was with Butler in his abortive attack on Fort Fisher; and served with W. T. Sherman in North Carolina as commander of the Third Division (Black troops) of the X Corps, and later, of the District of New Bern.

As commanding general, Paine led the Third Division of the X Corps at New Market Heights, found south of Richmond, Virginia. The Battle of New Market Heights resulted from Union General Ulysses S. Grant's campaign to capture the Confederate capital of Richmond. On September 29, 1864, Grant ordered Major General Benjamin F. Butler to move his Army north across the James River toward New Market Heights to penetrate the Confederate line. The X Corps and Third Division of the XVIII Corps would form the right wing of the assault and approach the Confederate line just south of New Market Road.

General Paine's soldiers, Third Division, XVIII Corps composed of USCT regiments, spearheaded the attack at New Market Heights. To reach the hilltop of the Confederate earthworks, USCT soldiers had to cross a rising plain with open fields, a marshy swamp along the bed of Four Mile Creek, and a thickly wooded ravine. Heavy Confederate artillery assaulted the USCT brigades as they continued their advance and eventually captured the hilltop.

During the entire Civil War, only sixteen Black soldiers received the Medal of Honor. The Army awarded fourteen of them to soldiers after the Battle of New Market Heights. All the medals awarded to Black soldiers during the war stemmed from one action and went to men of the Third Division, XVIII Corps, in the Army of the James. None of the medals for New Market Heights went to members of the black division of the X Corps. This is not surprising, for only three of the seventeen medals awarded to white troops for the action went to X Corps soldiers.

General Paine returned to civilian life with the brevet promotion of major general in 1866. Thereafter, he was an important, if unheralded, power in the development of the United States railroad network. He was a director of the Santa Fe, the Burlington, and the Mexican Central railroads.

Role of USCT Units in the New Market Heights Attack

The attack at New Market Heights forever sealed the fighting abilities and spirit of the Black soldier. The battle was part of a larger operation planned and directed by Union Major General Benjamin F. Butler. Besides New Market Heights, the XVIII and X Corps, composed of USCT regiments, fought at Fort Harrison, Fort Gilmer, and Laurel Hill during the same operation. Taken together, the events of September 29th and 30th are known as the Battle of Chaffin's Farm. It was the Union's most successful effort to break General Robert E. Lee's defensive lines north of the James River.

Early on the evening of September 28, Major General Butler called a council of war to give his commanders, Major General David Birney of the X Corps, Major General Edward O. C. Ord of the XVIII Corps and Cavalry Division commander Brigadier. General August V. Kautz, the details of the next operation. His plan called for two divisions of General Ord's XVIII Corps on the left wing to make a surprise crossing of the James River at Aiken's Landing and move up the Varnia Road to capture Confederate Fort Harrison. General Ord's forces would then wheel west and destroy the Confederate bridges at and above Chaffin's Bluff and race up the Osborn Turnpike for Richmond.

At precisely the same time, on the right wing, General Birney's X Corps, plus Brigadier General Charles J. Paine's USCT regiments detailed from the XVIII Corps, would cross the James River, advance from Deep Bottom, carry New Market Heights, and strike out for Richmond on the New Market Road. Finally, General Kautz's cavalry would move to the Darbytown Road and when the forces cleared New Market Heights would ride hard for the Confederate capital. General Butler convinced himself that the Black troops would fight and take a stronghold that confederate defenders denied the earlier Union attackers. Hence, he selected General Paine's Third Division of the XVIII Corps to spearhead the attack on New Market Heights.

At dawn on September 29th, Paine's division, made up of three all-USCT brigades, crossed the James River at Deep Bottom Landing. Their goal was to take New Market Heights. That would give them control of New Market Road, which led directly to Richmond.

Butler always expected that his attacks would catch the Confederates unaware. But the movements of so many men could hardly remain a secret, and by 4:00 a.m., the Confederate defenders of New Market Heights were already under arms and having a hot breakfast, awaiting the Union attackers. While the Confederates had breakfast, Union officers quietly moved through the darkness and ordered the exhausted men to wake up and stand-to-arms. General Paine's Black soldiers shouldered their muskets, smartly formed ranks, and passed through the defenses of Deep Bottom, heading north through the fog-shrouded pre-dawn darkness. Around 5:30 a.m., the crackling of musket fire announced that skirmishers of the 22nd Regiment USCT had opened the engagement by driving back the advance pickets.

According to historical reports of the battle, the soldiers the 4th and 6th Regiment USCT that followed had no way of knowing that the swampy terrain delayed most of the other Third Division units that were to be in the attack, so they were spearheading the attack on their own. The geography of the battlefield would continue to work against the attacking troops. To reach the Confederate earthworks, the USCT soldiers had to cross about five hundred yards on a rising plain. Four Mile Creek, across this plain, created a marshy swamp and a wooded ravine that ran parallel to the New Market Road. Beyond the ravine, another open plain of about three hundred yards sloped northward toward the road and the Confederate breastworks. As they advanced, the division came under heavy fire from Confederate earthwork defenses after the heavy losses, the Union forces withdrew.

Next, the Second Brigade, including the 5th, 36th, and 38th Regiment USCT, advanced. They also engaged in brutal fighting and lost over one-third of their forces before finding an opening and bursting through the Confederate line. After withstanding withering fire, the Confederate fire seemed to slacken. Union forces swept up the fragments of the Fourth and Sixth Regiment USCT, and the determined attackers surged forward into the Confederate positions. They advanced up New Market Heights while the Confederates retreated toward Richmond.

When the battle was over, soldiers from the USCT units proved their courage. Over and over, as the confederate defenders shot down Union color bearers and white commanding officers, Black soldiers stepped up to retrieve the colors and lead the troops. The efforts of the white officers and Black noncommissioned officers yielded success.

Thomas Morris Chester, a Black reporter for the Philadelphia Press, captivated by the role of the USCT regiments in combat, filed a dispatch focusing on their bravery. On October 5, he sent a dispatch from Richmond in which he declared that Brigadier General Charles J. Paine's Third Division of the XVIII Corps had covered itself with glory and wiped out effectively the imputation against the fighting qualities of colored troops.

Butler undertook his own project to overcome discrimination against Black troops. He designed a medal with the motto ferro iis libertas perveniet (freedom attained by the sword) and may have distributed two hundred of them. Yet geographical as well as racial factors were at work in the distribution of decorations. Soldiers in Virginia received the vast majority of Butler's medals.

Parson Worked Ferociously on the Escape Action Plan

When Parson resolved to escape bondage and run to freedom, it was a dangerous and potentially life-threatening decision. Escaping involved traveling a defined mission under harsh conditions and navigating into unknown territory while eluding slave catchers all made the journey perilous. Parson planned the escape based on the anticipation of early ground contact with slave catchers or patrollers, either en route or shortly after arrival at the destination. For Parson, the choice to leave behind his family and Frances, the target of his affection, was heart-wrenching and frustrating. He knew about the difficulties of surviving exposure to winter weather, hiding in swamps or wooded thickets, and navigating into unknown territory based on folklore methodologies.

Parson organized and started the quest with a clear vision of the escape plan from beginning to end-result. He assigned the roles and responsibilities to Joseph and Henry and rehearsed navigation methods. Parson analyzed the railroad map and marked out a route that helped navigation, gave advantage to friendly areas, and probable locations of adversaries.

Parson recognized the stakes were high, and he could only fulfill his vision with an achievable action plan. Parson assessed the risks, collected, and stored provisions, and gathered other equipment needed during his journey. Once he completed the plan, he revealed and designated tasks for each brother.

Chapter Eight
Quest for Freedom Behind Union Lines

By December 1864, a growing number of Parson's friends and acquaintances struck out for freedom, in part because so few white men remained behind in Southampton. Thousands of enslaved people escaped to the Union Army controlled areas, earning their freedom, and forcing the United States to develop a firm policy on emancipation. The long struggle to abolish slavery became a Civil War political aim and, in 1864, the greatest humanitarian undertaking in the nation's history.

According to information included the National Archives and Civil War pension applications for the First Cavalry Regiment, United States Colored Troops, Parson and his two brothers Joseph and Henry Sykes, alias Williams, liberated themselves from a Southampton County, Virginia plantation and "joined the Union Army at the same time and place." As recounted by oral family history, he planned an escape route that meandered along designated points along the railroad, starting in Cross Keys, through Boykins, Franklin, to Suffolk. During the Civil War, the Seaboard & Roanoke Railroad had depots and whistle stops from Weldon, North Carolina, through Boykins, to Portsmouth, Virginia, and finally into Norfolk.

During the Civil War, the Confederate government did not consider the Seaboard & Roanoke Railroad very important, especially after it abandoned Portsmouth in 1862. The government transferred the rolling stock and leased it to other more important railroads, including the company's primary competitor, the Petersburg Railroad. The government in Richmond ordered the railroad's iron striped and shipped to Manson, North Carolina, for the construction of an extension to the Roanoke Valley Railroad. Described next is a plausible rendition of Parson's heroic self-liberation ordeal.

Parson Sykes Alias Harrison Williams

As he matured into adulthood, Parson, now alias Harrison, developed a more sophisticated understanding of the premises of formal operational thought and actions needed to achieve their social, political, and economic goals. More than before, he remained unbendingly independent, hoping ultimately to liberate himself and brothers to start a free and prosperous life. He often thought of Frances, his love interest, and how she would resist the unwanted acts of intimacy of white slaveholders toward enslaved women during the rest of the war.

At sundown on December 2, 1864, Joseph and Henry met Parson at his haven, and retrieved their provisions, carpentry tools, network maps, and other equipment. Next, they quickly changed clothes to blend in with the terrain, assumed alias names, and started their quest easterly to the Blackwater River. While they knew the direction of travel by keeping the railroad tracks in view, they did not know exactly where they ended. However, they had a shared vision of the escape plan's end-result. They had just gotten away, relishing the thoughts of no longer having anyone telling them what to do, no one to claim them as property.

Led by Parson, the brothers started on their self-liberation ordeal, traveling east along the Seaboard & Roanoke Railroad. They towed their accumulation of provisions, carpentry tools, network maps, and other equipment and quickly changed clothes, assumed alias names, and continued their trip east to Norfolk. They knew the direction of travel by keeping the railroad tracks and telegraph lines in sight, but they did not know exactly where they went. Before leaving Southampton, they quickly changed clothes, assumed alias names, and continued their trip east, but did not know exactly where they were going.

The Transition from Jacob's Slave to a Butler's Contraband

Parson no longer thought of the brothers as slaves of Jacob Williams since they had transitioned into General Butler's contraband. The Emancipation Proclamation freed enslaved people in land controlled by the Confederate government, such as in Southampton County, Virginia. In August 1861, Congress approved the Confiscation Act and prompted the establishment of contraband communities such as Hampton, Virginia, known as the Grand Contraband Camp. While working at the depot, Parson found and read a newspaper article that stated Butler used the town of Hampton to house contraband and Union soldiers because of its proximity to Fort Monroe. It was the largest contraband community created by formerly enslaved people in Norfolk, Portsmouth, and York County. From there, seeking refuge in the Grand Contraband Camp on the Peninsula near Fort

Monroe, he hoped to enlist in the Union Army as members of the United States Colored Troops.

The status of being contraband offered a significant improvement over slavery, and many former slaves assumed it would eventually lead to full freedom. Starting in January 1863, many could gain their freedom by serving in all-Black regiments. In Kansas, some African Americans might even have joined the service as early as August 1862, when the 1st Kansas Colored Volunteers mustered into state service as the nation's first Black regiment before the federal government approved such units. Ratified on December 6, 1865, the 13th Amendment abolished slavery in the United States and all enslaved people finally gained full legal recognition as free citizens.

The Home Guard Patrol Encounter

After nightfall, the brother started on the self-liberation journey, the first segment traveling from the vicinity of Cross Keys to Newsoms, Virginia, without interruption. To manage the escape route, Parson divided the overall route into several smaller segments he could recognize. Each segment typically had only one Seaboard & Roanoke Railroad depot or whistle stop. Parson gave each segment a definite beginning and ending, marked with a control measure, such as a checkpoint or timeline. When possible, he matched the start and end points to a navigational aid or feature along the route.

The first segment of Parson's journey started at his haven and ended in Newsoms, Virginia, on the east bank of the Nottoway River. Parson suggested to Henry a pace to complete the segment in three hours. Parson planned stops in Newsoms and at the railroad bridge over the Nottoway

River to assess each situation. Earlier that day, Solomon warned him to check the areas along the way constantly for aggressive home guard patrols.

Under the cover of darkness, Parson and his brothers started the escape plan east toward the Union Army controlled territory across the Blackwater River. They zigzagged through the stacks of peanuts in the field into the forest. The men moved to and from as much of the concealed positions as available into the forest and meandered to Boykins.

Arriving at Boykins, Parson selected a secure hollow on the west bank of the Nottoway River to check the area for the avenues of escape and for evidence of the home guard patrols. The men traveled along familiar pig paths in the forest past Boykins to Newsoms, on high alert to identify obstacles and determine adverseness.

As they plunged deeper into the wooded forest toward Newsoms, they believed and felt that they would be safe from capture and came to rest in a slight clearing, and each brother took turns watching. As Parson completed his watch, he heard footsteps in the bushes, but before he could react, a two-man home guard patrol approached him. Parson recognized the men in the patrol from working in the depot.

Before the patrollers started their interrogation, Parson performed a quick rouse to neutralize suspicion, by showing them an old pass signed by Caswell, allowing the brothers to be away from his plantation at night in Cross Keys. Once the guards reviewed and returned the pass, the brothers quickly ran away from the older and slower men and plunged deeper into the wooded forest, heading east to the Nottoway River railroad bridge.

They dashed through familiar walking trails toward the railroad bridge over the Nottoway River. After checking the areas out for additional home guard patrols, Joseph navigated the escapees safely crossing the Nottoway River and through the forest, avoiding detection. Parson secured a place on the east bank of the river to inspect the area and his immediate surroundings.

The Slave Catchers Encounter

On the east side of the Nottoway River, west of the Blackwater River and closer to the Union line, Parson stopped near Delaware, Virginia, to check the area, find obstacles, and assess adverseness. Solomon warned Parson that the citizens east of the Nottoway formed vigilante slave catchers to patrol and control their slaves, to enforce the enslavement codes, and regulate slave behavior. The hired slave catchers had three primary duties, including catching runaways along Blackwater and Nottoway Rivers, dispersing slave gatherings, and safeguarding white communities.

Sternly warned of aggressive slave catchers patrolling in the area, Parson moved in closer to see the territory and find evidence of slave catchers. As he meandered through the bushy vegetation, Parson heard footsteps behind and to his rear. As he hid in the bushes, a two-man slave catcher patrol that had been looking for escapees apprehended him. The slave catchers had already apprehended Joseph and Henry and were interrogating them. According to an oral family anecdote, as the patrollers questioned the brothers, Harrison offered them plugs of tobacco. When the patrollers grabbed the tobacco, the brothers attacked, overpowered, stabbed, and killed one of them, and injured the other. After the deadly scuffle, the men hastily zigzagged through the forest toward the Blackwater River.

Around midnight, the tired and exhausted brothers reached the Franklin Depot. After visually inspecting the immediate surrounding from a secure point, the men meandered around the depot and checked out the bridge crossing the Blackwater River. Not seeing any local citizens, slave catchers or confederate soldiers guarding the area, the men dashed across the bridge over the Blackwater River, the demarcation of the Union forces and the Confederate defensive line.

After traveling all night and safely across the Blackwater River inside Union controlled Nansemond County, Parson and his companions moved further inside the county to as much of a concealed position as they could find. Next, they set up a camouflaged bivouac area in the forest to rest, eat, and took turns napping.

The Encounter with a Black Union Scout

Before sunrise on December 3, the men rose, broke camp, and hurried out toward Carrsville. After meandering around the town, they rested briefly in the surrounding Nansemond County Forest. While on his watch, Henry saw a Black man romping through the forest and quickly alerted Parson, who greeted the man, and discovered that he was a former slave and a scout for Brigadier General Edward A. Wild. He said USCT scouts were out on expeditions in all directions, some seeking recruits and contraband families, some collecting forage, and some gathering firewood.

The scout told Parson that General Wild was commander of a Black infantry brigade known as "Wild's African Brigade." The brigade, headquartered in Norfolk, included men from the 36th and 37th United States Colored Troops. He told the brothers that Gen Wild's raid into confederate territory was the first of any size undertaken by Black troops since the Congress allowed their enlistment and ended the question of their efficiency in any branch of the service. He said General Wild believed his raid was successful, and it freed 2,500 enslaved people by his estimation.

As they parted company, the scout informed Parson that there were only a few confederate soldiers along the banks of the Blackwater River. He said all the Confederate cavalries had been ordered to Petersburg. He informed Parson that around Suffolk City and in Norfolk County, there were confederate guerrillas, border states, slave catchers, and vigilante patrollers guarding white neighborhoods intensely.

Encounter with United States Military Railroad Black Laborers

After leaving the area around Carrsville, the brothers approached Buckhorn, a major stop for the railway. In the forest outside of Buckhorn, the brothers came upon a mud and timber dwelling built by a migratory Black woodcutter near the railroads. Parson met and greeted the man who the Union Army employed to chop timber for railroad ties and bridges and fuel for military locomotives.

As Union forces gained control of confederate territories, enslaved Black people contacted them to escape enslavement. Much of this contact between Union forces and escapees took place along the railroads. As Black people joined and signed up for the USCT, many ended up in the United States Military Railroads, Construction Corps. Stationed at remote camps, migratory woodcutter also faced the constant danger of Confederate pickets and guerrilla raids.

As they parted company, the man was very accommodating, readily giving the brothers forage and rations. He warned the brothers to watch for and evade Confederate pickets and guerrilla raiders working around Suffolk City.

The Confederate Guerrilla Threat Around Suffolk

In 1863, the Confederate government placed Lieutenant General James Longstreet in command of its Department of Virginia and North Carolina. They gave Longstreet four objectives: 1) to protect Richmond, 2) give support to Robert E. Lee's Army of Northern Virginia if needed, 3) forage and gather supplies for the Confederate armies, and 4) to capture the Union garrison at Suffolk if possible. Longstreet had three divisions of troops from the Army of Northern Virginia and North Carolina.

General Longstreet had completely succeeded in two of his original objectives: foraging and protecting Richmond. However, he did not capture any of the Union garrison at Suffolk. Since that time, Confederates defending along the Blackwater River continued a guerrilla war against the occupying Union forces in Nansemond County and garrison at Suffolk.

On April 29, 1864, General Robert E. Lee directed Longstreet to disengage from Suffolk and rejoin the Army of Northern Virginia at Fredericksburg. By May 4, the last of Longstreet's units had crossed the Blackwater River en route to Richmond, leaving behind a small detachment of. Confederate pickets and guerrilla raiders. Throughout the rest of the Civil War, the confederates continuously crossed the Blackwater River to forage, scout, and harass the Union troops and sympathizers.

Encounter with Border States Fugitive Slaves Hunters

As the sun set on December 3, the men approached Magnolia, a whistle stop for the railway east of Suffolk. The men bivouacked for the night about two and a half miles beyond the Magnolia stop, in a secured and camouflaged area. Before sunrise the next morning, they resumed their march watchfully to avoid meeting any fugitive-slave hunters.

The militia-style border states fugitive slave hunters hoped to seize runaways and return them to a farm in Maryland for a reward. Like the Confederate states, border states relied heavily on slave labor and feared that emancipation of slavery would disrupt the economic status quo. When the Confederate states seceded, President Lincoln continued to enforce the Fugitive Slave Law. Lincoln did this to keep the slave–holding border states in the Union. In 1864, Fugitive Slave Patrols captured and returned runaway slaves to their owners in states loyal to the Union. The patrols had the authority to control and deny access to equal rights for freed slaves. They relentlessly and systematically enforced Black Codes, strict local and state laws that regulated and restricted access to labor, wages, voting rights, and general freedoms for formerly enslaved people.

Fugitive Slave Patrols continued into early 1865, near the end of the war. The acts remained in effect until the 13th Amendment passed and abolished slavery in the United States. Congress passed the amendment on January 31, 1865, and ratified it on December 6, 1865.

During his encounter with the border state's fugitive slave hunters, Parson successfully convinced them he and his brothers were from Southampton, Virginia and not Maryland, a slave–holding border state in the Union. The patrollers released the men to pursue their ordeal along the Seaboard & Roanoke Railroad.

USCT Recruiters and Pickets from Camp Bowers Hill

On the morning of December 4, 1864, the brothers came upon the Union forces that occupied Camp Foster Bowers Hill, Virginia, in Norfolk County, on the Seaboard & Roanoke Railroad, at a point about equally distant between Portsmouth, opposite Norfolk, and Suffolk. The Union pickets at Camp Bowers Hill blocked the approach of Confederate forces west of Suffolk attacks upon the ports of Norfolk and Portsmouth from the Blackwater River.

For Union forces, Camp Bowers Hill was in a convenient location and provided an effective means to help defend the railroads, particularly the Norfolk and Petersburg Railroad. The Western Branch to its head made a natural boundary and controlled with relative ease aggression from the northwest. The Union recognized this and constructed a picket line to help control the eastern seaboard from the Western Branch of the Elizabeth River to North Carolina's Roanoke Island and the Albemarle Sound.

The brothers, as contraband, made their way to the Camp Bowers Hill picket line and volunteered for the Union Army. General Butler of the Army of the James was recruiting freed men to fill the USCT Regiments for the Department of Virginia and North Carolina in Norfolk City. Upon recruitment by the Union Army, the picket sent them to the Provost Marshal for muster into the Company I, 1st Regiment United States Colored Cavalry.

Major General Edward Otho Cresap Ord - XVIII Corps

Before Parson entered military service, he heard of Major General Edward Otho Cresap Ord's leadership of Black soldiers during the Petersburg Campaign. A career United States Army officer, Edward O. C. Ord played major leadership roles in both theaters of the American Civil War and as commander of the Department of the Arkansas at the conclusion of hostilities. Parson proudly retold stories at family gatherings about Major General Ord's leadership of the Army of the James.

Major General Ord received an appointment to the United States Military Academy at sixteen years in 1835. Among his classmates were Henry Halleck and Edward R.S. Canby, both of whom became general officers in the U.S. Army during the American Civil War. Ord graduated from the Academy on July 1, 1839, placing the seventeenth in his class of thirty-one cadets. At the outbreak of the Civil War, Ord was a brigade commander of the Pennsylvania Reserves.

On May 3, 1862, the Union Army promoted Ord to major general, and commander of the 2nd Division of the Army of the Tennessee. He missed serving during the Battle of Corinth but took part in the end of the Siege of Vicksburg. He briefly commanded the XIII Corps with the Department of the Gulf, after which he went to the eastern theater in 1864 to command the XVIII Corps.

Ord commanded the XVIII Corps at the siege of Richmond. He sustained serious wounds in the attack on Fort Harrison in September 1864. In January 1865, he assumed command of the Army of the James, as well as the Department of North Carolina.

During the Battle of the Crater, while Ord's forces were available, they did not actively take part. In late 1864, the XVIII Corps took part in an attack on Fort Harrison.

When Richmond, Virginia fell on April 2, 1865, Ord as commander of the Army of the James indirectly led the Black soldiers of the 25th Corps that were among the first Union troops to occupy the city on the following day. At Appomattox, the 24th Corps assigned to the Army of the James cut off the Army of Northern Virginia's last avenue of escape, prompting Robert E. Lee's surrender on April 9, 1865.

As the Civil War ended, the Army brevetted Ord to the rank of brigadier-general in the regular army for gallant and meritorious services at the battle of the Hatchie's Bridge and to major general in the regular army for gallant and meritorious services at the assault of Fort Harrison. Both promotions were effective on March 13, 1865.

At the conclusion of hostilities, the U.S. War Department issued General Orders No. 118 on June 27, 1865, which divided the United States into military districts and divisions. The order placed Ord in command of the Department of the Ohio, headquartered in Detroit. Ord assumed his new command on July 5, 1865, and served until August 6, 1866. During his tenure with the Department of the Ohio, the War Department promoted him to lieutenant colonel in the regular army on December 11, 1865, and to brigadier-general in the regular army on July 26, 1866. On August 29, 1866, the department assigned Ord to command the Department of Arkansas.

As the commander of the department, Ord ensured Arkansas followed federal laws. Serving as the assistant commissioner of the Freedmen's Bureau, he worked to protect former slaves from attack. He worked to improve working relationships between landowners and the former slaves. While he protected the formerly enslaved people from abuse and violence, he also ordered his agents to force the workers to fulfill their contracts with plantation owners. He successfully increased the number of schools for formerly enslaved people in Arkansas.

Throughout his career, Ord proved himself to be a resourceful, brave, and aggressive commander. General Grant overlooked his few flaws and brought the best out in him during some of the Union Army's greatest campaigns.

The Role of USCT in the Battle of Fort Harrison

The greatest number of USCT regiments served in the Virginia theater as part of General Grant's operations, fighting around Petersburg and Richmond in the last two years of the war. Referring to several combat missions which occurred near this city, Secretary of War Edwin Stanton asserted, "The hardest fighting was done by the Black troops. The forts they stormed were the worst of all."

As reported by Civil War correspondents, alongside New Market Heights, the assault on Fort Harrison formed the second distinct stage at the Battle of Chaffin's Farm. Fort Harrison stood as a critical link in Richmond's defenses, which therefore made it a tempting target for the Army of the James under General Benjamin F. Butler.

On September 29, 1864, Fort Harrison was the strongest part of the defense because of its strategic placement with clear site lines toward the James River. With only 1,750 Confederates in the fort compared to the 4,150 Union soldiers that surrounded them, the Fort quickly fell. USCT troops from Major General David B. Birney's X Corps and Major General Edward O. C. Ord's XVIII Corps were present at Chaffin's Farm. After the confederates critically wounded General Ord in the altercation and he could not command for several months.

General Lee knew the importance of Fort Harrison and tried to recapture it the following day. On September 30, Robert E. Lee organized a major effort to retake the lost fort. His attack also lacked coordination, and the well-prepared Union defenders, some of them armed with multiple shot weapons, crushed the Confederate effort, and inflicted a significant loss on the attackers. Robert E. Lee ordered a counterattack to retake Fort Harrison, now commanded by Major General Godfrey Weitzel, replacing the wounded General Ord. The Confederate attacks were uncoordinated and easily repulsed.

Black journalist Thomas Morris Chester wrote that the USCT men had "covered [themselves] with glory and wiped out effectually the imputation against the fighting qualities of the colored troops." Even Lee recognized the size of the victory, telling one of his generals, expecting a quick victorious reprisal, "I made my effort this morning and failed, losing many men killed and wounded. I have another line provided for that point and shall have no more bloodshed at the fort unless you can show me a practical plan of capture; perhaps you can. I shall be glad to have it."

Parson and His Brothers Successfully Escaped Jacob's Farm

Parson realized to achieve the goal, he needed an actionable plan that had stipulated readiness and preparation on short notice to overcome the hardship, danger, and difficulty of escaping from slavery. He understood how to navigate in the terrain based on methods allegedly practiced by Nat Turner to figure out his location and direction, to stay on the right path, and to tell the time of day. He prepared a plan to achieve the difficult goal of fleeing Jacob's domination.

During the journey, for every step forward, it seemed the brothers took two steps back. Parson's setbacks began even before he goes to the haven. He had trouble not retrieving the memory of Jacob's treatment and warning that living under Union control would not be better. He battled with slave patrollers, Confederate guerrillas, and Border States Fugitive Slaves Hunters. Often, as he tried to solve one of these issues, he failed. Even when he finally conquered one problem, another arose.

Parson's journey to cross Union lines incurred enormous risks. His flight was a tremendous gamble. He did not know the exact location of the Union army, and nearly fell into the hands of Confederate guerrillas or citizens. The consequences of either were grave. To avoid detection, Parson traveled by night and hid during the daylight hours, getting food from fellow Black people or foraging as best he could.

Parson and his brothers successfully entered Union occupied territory, exhausted and ravenous. With the guarantee of three meals a day, clothing, shelter, and pay, enlistment in the army was their only means of support. Union regiments recruited soldiers and created companies in the occupied territory. Given the leadership qualities Parson displayed, that the curiously young slave had become a matured and skillful leader.

Chapter Nine
Behold, Comrades-in-Arms!

On that chilly morning in December 1864, the Sykes brothers completed Parson's escape plan east toward Norfolk County, Virginia. The next morning at daybreak, Union pickets and recruiters from the Provost Marshal of the Army of the James stopped the three men near or at Camp Bowers Hill, Virginia. Jacob Williams' greatest fear had come real, Black men with guns, who not only did not look like slaves anymore but more like comrades-in-arms.

At Fort Monroe, Major General Benjamin F. Butler applied his pioneering experience with the first Black regiments mustered into Union military service. He organized the new 10th Regiment, United States Colored Infantry, which recruited 1,000 refugee slaves from the crowded contraband camps near Camp Hamilton in Hampton, Newport News, Old Point Comfort, and Craney Island. Two new regiments of black cavalry, the First and the Second, formed at Camp Hamilton and Fort Monroe on December 22, 1863, followed by Battery B of the 2nd United States Colored Light Artillery at Fort Monroe on January 8, 1864.

Parson and his brothers safely arrived at Camp Bowers Hill in Norfolk County. Bower's Hill was in Virginia, on the Seaboard

& Roanoke Railroad line, at a point about equidistance between Portsmouth, opposite Norfolk, and Suffolk. Eager Union recruiters greeted them as they entered the camp. Within those contraband camps where enslaved people used the army as their shield to freedom, General Butler recruited enough Black recruits to fill several Union regiments.

For the brothers, the first contact with Union Army personnel was breathtaking moments. They had stepped forward in their country's time of need, and the nation accepted them readily. For the first time, they felt as if they were on the same level as whites.

During the war, however, Black troops also faced a different battle—a battle against discrimination in pay, promotions, and medical care. General Butler directed his men to treat Black soldiers with respect and declared his opposition to the government's policy of paying African American soldiers less than white soldiers. This checked the worst abuses, but there were still frustrating ordeals to overcome before Parson achieved his goal.

First Cavalry Regiment, United States Colored Troops

Parson and his brothers enrolled into the Company I, First Cavalry Regiment, United States Colored Troops. During the Civil War, the Union Army accepted Black soldiers into companies until battalions and regiments filled the personnel requirements, after which the Adjutant General numbered the regiments in the order raised. The Army organized the First Cavalry Regiment, USCT at Camp Hamilton, Virginia. When Parson enrolled in December 1864, the regiment was a unit of the 1st Brigade, 3rd Division, 18th Corps, Army of the James. In the Union Army, an average of four regiments joined to make a brigade. This size unit had approximately 4,000 men and a brigadier general as its commander.

On July 15, 1863, the United States War Department issued General Order No. 217, combining the Department of Virginia with the Department of North Carolina to form the Department of Virginia and North Carolina, and appointed Major General John G. Foster to command the new department. Troops from these departments formed the XVIII Corps.

Initially, the XVIII Corps had five divisions stationed in North Carolina, making it one of the largest in the Union, and placed under the command of General John G. Foster. By August 1863, most of the corps' original units were disbanded or transferred elsewhere, while the War Department re-designated the bulk of the discontinued VII Corps from Virginia as the XVIII Corps. In April 1864, the War Department transferred the X Corps from the Department of the South, and the two corps formed the Army of the James.

When first organized, the Army of the James recruited eligible men from among the counties located nearby the Virginia Peninsula. The attrition of disease, combat, and desertion rapidly reduced the number of men in the command. Individual replacements were rare; hence, it was more typical to raise an entirely new regiment instead. The commander handled operational and administrative duties for the regiment and led his regiment into battle personally to ensure that it performed to its utmost ability.

A few months later, on October 28, 1863, the War Department issued General Order No. 350, appointing Major General Benjamin F. Butler to command the department and the XVIII Army Corps. Butler arrived at Fort Monroe, Virginia, and assumed command on November 10, 1863.

Later, on April 12, 1864, Grant instructed Butler to collect all the forces from his command that he could spare from garrison duty to work on the south side of the James River, Richmond being his end. The forces under Butler's command were known as the Army of the James thereafter. In the Union, an army included from one to eight corps and typically named after an important river or waterway. A major general commanded an army by issuing instructions on strategic objectives and operational requirements to his corps commanders on where to deploy their divisions.

During the spring of 1864, the War Department transferred the corps—now commanded by General William Farrar Smith, formerly of VI Corps—to Yorktown, Virginia, to join Maj. Gen. Benjamin Butler's Army of the James. The corps played a major part in the unsuccessful operations in the Bermuda Hundred and was also heavily engaged at Cold Harbor. On June 12, Lt. Gen. Ulysses S. Grant sent Smith on a surprise march to seize Petersburg from the Confederate forces before Robert E. Lee could mention the bulk of the Army of Northern Virginia. In the Second Battle of Petersburg, June 15–18, 1864, Smith made successful initial attacks against the outnumbered defenses of Gen. P. G. T. Beauregard; but after driving Beauregard's men from their outer entrenchments on the 15th, Smith, fearful of a Confederate counterattack, lost his nerve and did not press the attack when it could have resulted in the easy seizure of the city.

In early December 1864, when Parson arrived, 1st Regiment United States Colored Troops Cavalry was a unit in the 1st Brigade, 4th Division, IX Corps, commanded by Brigadier General Edward Ferrero. Between the 1st Regiment USCT's arrival in Portsmouth on July 1, 1863, and the creation of the Army of the James the following April, the army recruited, trained, and embarked more than a dozen USCT regiments on their first operations in Hampton Roads. Ultimately, they not only formed the nucleus of the Union's first all-black XXV Army corps, but they also earned fame as its first Union Army troops to enter Richmond.

The XXV Army Corps the Largest Black Unit in the Civil War

On December 3, 1864, the War Department reorganized two Union commands, the X Corps and the XVIII Corps, to form two racially segregated units. White units became the XXIV Corps, and the Black units became the XXV Corps. The XXV Corps was the single largest Black unit of the Union Army during the American Civil War and the only all-Black Army corps in United States military history. The XXV Corps had approximately 13,630 troops, including infantry, cavalry, and artillery units, commanded by Major General Godfrey Weitzel. This was significant because the XXIV Corps and the XXV Corps made up an army sized in the Civil War on December 3, 1864.

The new XXV Corps had three divisions. The division unit leaders were General A. Kautz (First Division), General William Birney (Second Division), and General Charles Paine (Third Division). Its white officers led Black soldiers. Union forces, under the overall command of General Ulysses S. Grant, intensified their pursuit of the Confederate troops.

Later in December, Grant ordered Butler to lead a provisional corps of his army in an assault on Fort Fisher, which guarded the port of Wilmington, North Carolina, the Confederacy's last major Atlantic seaport. Operating with Rear Admiral David D. Porter, Butler troops began landing near the fort following a naval bombardment of over 10,000 shells. After setting up a beachhead, Butler incurred Grant's wrath when he called off the operation after deciding that the shelling had not damaged the fort enough to capture it.

Lacking confidence in Butler's leadership, Grant appealed to President Lincoln and Secretary of War Stanton for authorization to replace Butler. On January 7, 1865, the Adjutant-General's Office issued General Order Number 1, which said in part that, "By direction of the President of the United States, Major General Benjamin F. Butler is relieved from the command of the Department of North Carolina and Virginia." On the same day, U.S. Army Headquarters issued special orders appointing Major General Edward Ord to temporary command of the Department and of the Army of the James.

Union Pickets and Recruiters from the Provost Marshal

The regiment Provost Marshal enforced camp discipline. His functions included supporting the camp jail and supervising the guards furnished daily by line regiments in rotation. From Camp Bowers Hill, the three brothers arrived at the Provost Marshal's office at Fort Norfolk, the base of supplies for the Army of the James, and for the Union establishments. Union pickets stop the three men near or at Fort Norfolk, and regimental recruiter enlisted them into the Union Army as carpenters.

The next day, a sharply uniformed black guard from the Provost Marshal's office escorted Parson and other comrades-in-arms on a steamship to join the Company I, 1st Regiment Cavalry, XXV Corps at Fort Monroe on the Virginia Peninsula. The guard sailed with the three men across the Chesapeake Bay to begin the enrollment and complete basic training at Fort Hamilton with other Black recruits from Virginia and North Carolina.

During enrollment, Parson always showed his ardent desire for freedom, and welcomed the pickets and guards from the Provost Marshal's office as liberators. He, by serendipity, eluded and evaded the many unscrupulous civilian and military recruiters who defrauded men of enlistment bounties, lied to them, and accepted men for service, with obvious illnesses, injuries, wounds, or deformities.

Parson Sykes in His Blue Uniform

The first step was a physical examination to evaluate the fitness for service. For admission into the army, each of the brothers divested themselves of all clothing, and the examiner checked for soundness or unsoundness by causing them to jump, bend over, kick, receive sundry thumps in the chest and back, and such other tests, as necessary. The examiners checked their teeth and evaluated the brothers' eyesight. After they passed, each received a passing authorization to continue to the next station.

Next, all three brothers moved toward and entered the recruiting station. There they signed the roll of Company I in which they enrolled, left descriptions, including height, complexion, and occupation, and then went to the examining surgeon, and again subjected to a critical examination. After Parson became a soldier, the Provost Marshal sent him at once to training camp, with instructions granting a short furlough to tour the town.

Parson and his brothers were glad to be members of the 1st Regiment United States Colored Troops Cavalry battle unit. The regimental commander supervised the enlistment process and served as the recruits' commanding officer. Because this officer commanded the recruits, and perhaps even entered battle with them, it behooved the officer to treat the men responsibly. Usually, a colonel led the command and had administrative duties for the regiment. In this role, the Army expected him to lead his regiment into battle personally to ensure that it performed to its utmost ability. For this reason, opposing forces defenders often killed or wounded colonels in action.

Black and White Comrades-in-arms

At the beginning of the Civil War, Jacob Williams did not believe that the United States would need his slave labor to support their military effort, particularly since it was a white man's war. He reasoned the Union would refuse to use black recruits, because rejecting them showed it was a war to preserve the Union, including slavery and all. War in a democracy requires the support of many of its citizens.

As Parson continued his self-liberation quest, he met and befriended other black recruits, who served with him throughout the rest of the war. He worked with hundreds of comrades in the blue uniforms aligned in the regiment, mostly indistinguishable from one another. He grew a strong bond with some soldiers in his company unit, such as the other former slaves from the Cross Keys, and the freed Black men who ran farms in Southampton County before the Civil War. Parson was glad Joseph and Henry embarked on the journey to Fort Monroe to achieve self-liberation. While Francis did not escape with Parson, she served a critical role in helping him see himself as a man of unbending independence, ultimately hopes to liberate himself and others inside and out of military service. Throughout the reminder of his military service, Parson kept contact with her and his parents by mail.

As documented in the Civil War archives, Parson served with many undifferentiated companions in the First Cavalry Regiment from Southampton County, Virginia. Comrade Henry Charity, enlisted in Company E, First Cavalry Regiment, United States Colored Troops. A close friend of Parson, he enlisted near the beginning of the war in Southampton County. According to public records, in 1850, a Southampton County, Virginia family included Gincy Charity, head of household and presumptive mother of six children, and an adult male. All were free Black people. At the time of Henry Charity's enlistment, Gincy Charity received the pay for each son if they remained hired out and that it was actually necessary for Gincy Charity's support.

Comrade Joshua Charity, enlisted in Company A, First Cavalry Regiment, United States Colored Troops. Before enlistment, this soldier and his free born brothers hired themselves out to support their mother in Southampton County, Virginia.

Comrade Thomas Charity, enlisted in Company E, First Cavalry Regiment, United States Colored Troops. The War Department paid him three hundred dollars advance bounty money when he entered and transferred him to Fort Powhatan. There he died early in the spring of 1865. He died in the United States Hospital from a disease contracted in the Army.

Comrade Friday Charity alias Friday Whipple, enlisted in Company I, 2nd United States Colored Cavalry. This comrade fled his apprenticeship and enlisted in the Union Army. He died of "congestive fever" (malaria) in a regimental hospital.

Comrade Jacob Sugars, enlisted in Company I, First Cavalry Regiment, United States Colored Troops. Jacob Sugars was born enslaved in Southampton County years after the 1831 Nat Turner Rebellion in that county.

Chaplain Garland H. White, Parson's Moral Guide and Adviser

At an early age, Parson inherited strong religious beliefs from his parents. One story he enjoyed telling was about his encounter with Chaplain Garland H. White. Parson met Chaplain White at Fort Monroe where he performed courageous services for Black soldiers and for their country, even when others mistreated and unappreciated them outside of the army. He learned a lot from Chaplain White and amusingly retold the story at family gatherings.

Chaplain Garland H. White was one of the few Black Union officers in the Civil War. After escaping slavery to Ontario, he became a minister in the African Methodist Episcopal Church. Chaplain White returned to the United States to preach and to recruit Black soldiers. The War Department assigned him to the all-black 4th Division, commanded by Brigadier General Edward Ferrero in the trenches before Petersburg fortification. Joining the division as a private in late 1863, he hoped to become unit chaplain. During this time, he continued to recruit for the regiment, mostly former slaves from Virginia and Maryland.

To Parson, Chaplain White reminded him of Nat Turner as he used the historic slave revolt to symbolize the principles of self-determination. The basic points of his sermons were to tell Black soldiers that racism and slavery were a major cause of the civil war and the Black uprisings in the past represented ongoing political, economic, and moral war. Chaplain White preached that Black people, based on the principles of self-determination, equal rights, and fair equality of opportunity, have the natural duty to select, choose and pursue their social, economic, and political status without interference. He argued against laws, movements, and violent discourse that keep Black people enslaved within restricted social, economic, and political boundaries.

Chaplain White impressed Parson with his advocacy of the principles of self-determination. He advocated private property ownership, economic freedom, and political support of the United States constitution. However, racism and discrimination continue to permeate all aspects of Black people's circumstances because of the unchecked existence of and emergence of white supremacy groups that looked to keep Black people within restricted social, economic, and political boundaries. Despite all this, at the heart of self-determination was help from a stoic guide and adviser who believes in other's dreams.

Chaplain White took it upon himself to function as a schoolteacher for Parson and other soldiers with little or no formal education. Since there were several formerly enslaved people serving in the military, this work was also important. With the rudiments of an education, such as reading and writing, these soldiers could work better in the world that did not totally accept them. Chaplain White taught anyone who wanted to learn. He taught them such subjects as English, reading, writing, and arithmetic. Chaplain White used various methods and techniques to raise interest in the reading and writing project.

USCT Soldiers Proved Their Gallantry in the Assault on Fort Gilmer

Some white officers questioned the fighting abilities of Black troops, but in the assault on Fort Gilmer, soldiers from the 9th United States Colored Troops silenced the doubters. The attack on Fort Gilmer played a prominent role in repulsing the Union to drive north toward Richmond. During the fighting on September 29, 1864, Fort Gilmer was yet another instance in which USCT Black soldiers proved their gallantry, getting farther with four companies than an entire division had been able to just hours earlier.

Fought late in the day, this battle came about because of the success achieved by Major General David Bell Birney's X Corps at New Market Heights. As Birney's troops pushed westward up the New Market Road toward Richmond after the battle, the lead division came under heavy artillery fire from Fort Gilmer. After some hemming and hawing, the division commanders considered it unwise to continue toward Richmond with such a powerful fort in their rear. They concluded their forces had to take in Fort Gilmer.

While most historians recount the fighting that took place at New Market Heights, there is another encounter involving USCT regiments that took place on the same day that merits examination—the Battle of Fort Gilmer.

The first assault column was ready to go by 12:50 p.m. but did not receive the order to attack until 1:2 p.m. Ten minutes later, 1,400 men of Brigadier General Robert S. Foster's Second Division moved forward. The line of advance would take them into the sights of Confederate gunners before they moved across three separate ravines that threw off their alignment and caused great confusion among the ranks. After they crossed the third ravine, they appeared in an open field that was directly in front of the fort. If they could make it across that field, they would meet one line of sharpened stakes sticking chest high out of the ground and one line of sharpened branches of treetops interlocked together to form an early barbed wire and then a ditch, or moat, that was ten feet deep. If by a miracle they could surmount these obstacles, they would then have to climb up the wall of the fort and fight their way in. General Foster's men—who would wind up attacking the fort twice—did not take the fort.

As the day wore on, the USCT Brigade, under the command of Brigadier General William Birney (the corps commander's older brother) arrived. Since General Foster's division had failed twice, the corps commander decided that Brigadier General William Birney's brigade would attack next. He unfortunately threw his men in piecemeal. With two regiments pinned down or withdrawing from the field, a garbled order came down from brigade that the 7th USCT was to attack the fort with only four companies. Fort Gilmer would not fall on September 29th. The 7th USCT lost twenty killed, eighty-two wounded, and 133 missing.

Paine's Division of the XVIII Corps and Birney's Colored Division of the X Corps were conspicuously engaged at Chaffin's Farm, in the assault on Fort Gilmer and the entrenchments at New Market Heights. At Fort Gilmer, they scaled the parapet by climbing upon each other's backs. A distinguished rebel general wrote at the time: "Fort Gilmer proved the other day that they would fight."

Parson and his Brothers Became Involved in the Civil War

Jacob Williams did not believe that the United States would need his slave labor to support their military effort and would refuse to use black recruits. He was wrong. War in a democracy requires the support of all its citizens. On Parson's behalf, his clear visualization, skillful researching, operational planning, and moral principles built on human rights got him to his destination. When the Union pickets stopped them near or at Fort Norfolk, Parson and brothers became involved in the civil war. The regimental recruiter enlisted them into the Union Army as carpenters.

After Parson became a soldier, the provost marshal sent him at once to training camp and granted him a short furlough to tour the town. Once in uniform, however, things were not so simple for Parson and his brothers. Even as they served their country, Black soldiers would encounter to several kinds of discrimination. Often, their units commanders assigned them to menial labor, refused to employ them in combat, and often they had to use inferior equipment. While more than a hundred Black men were officers, none reached a level higher than the rank of major. If captured by Confederate forces, Black soldiers risked re-enslavement or executed.

Once in uniform, Parson joined his squad and met his corporal and sergeant. He quickly learned the correct way to stand, to turn, and to get from one place to another and that someone would still tell him what to do. When Parson joined the First Cavalry Regiment, USCT, he thought he would ride a horse instead of marching and thus have a comfortable time in the army. This idea quickly vanished with lessons on how to march and to execute facing commands.

Parson committed to pursue self-liberation and entered the Union Army to fight for freedom is steps closer. He skillfully planned his self-liberation ordeal to reach Fort Monroe alive and fit for military service. He and his two brothers solidified their commitment to the call for self-liberation and to enter the fight for human rights. Their aims to gain desired ends via self-determination, and to create ways and means of uplifting from their rock bottom economic conditions remains for him to achieve.

Epilogue

After the Civil War, for the next 150 years or more at Sykes' family reunions, holiday meals, weddings, and other gatherings, Parson's descendants discussed and recalled how he and his brothers escaped from enslavement and enlisted in the Union Army. Sykes' family elders were vital resources for their recollections, wisdom, and guidance. They gave the strength, empowerment, and motivation for the tight family network that continues from generation to generation. Self-liberation was the beginning of the Parson's struggle to secure human rights and equality for all Americans.

As December 1864 ended, Parson had successfully self-liberated himself and enrolled for military service in the Union Army. Next, he completed basic training at Fort Hamilton, then sailed on a steamship up the James River and joined the rest of the 1st Cavalry Regiment (USCT) at City Point, Virginia. A little over three months later, he accompanied USCT regiments that entered and led the capture of Richmond, Virginia, which for the past four years, served as the capital of the Confederacy. During their military service, inequalities plagued the Sykes brothers as they served and fought in segregated USCT regiments.

Conspicuously squelched in American history, however, is the recognition, distinction and honor rarely extolled on Parson and his comrades-in-arms for leading Union units into Richmond. This undiscovered historic information is available in stacks of little used documents at National Archives and Records Administration (NARA), the nation's record keeper. Despite the proven effective, courageous, and victorious combat record USCT regiments, Parson and his comrades-in-arms still faced a long struggle for equal treatment.

Parson Sykes - Early Adulthood

Parson realized that the Union Army offered a rare opportunity for Black men to prove to the world how they contributed significantly to the Union in times of crisis and to gaining their own freedom. As the Civil War raged on in its last year, Parson continually undermined the validity of the Confederate cause, promoted the abolition movement, and unceasing resistance to enslavement. He grew into a well-disciplined soldier, lived by his convictions, and grew into a charismatic local leader. Self-liberation gave meaning and joy to his life, and he never abandoned the pursuit of full citizenship, even while knowing the endless resistance and the obstacles that confronted him.

While growing into early adulthood, Parson planned and successfully conducted his self-liberation from Jacob Williams' farm in Southampton County. In planning and preparing for self-liberation, he considered vision, direction, guidance, coordination, and logistic coherence. After self-liberation, he never again feared that the Fugitive Slave catchers would apprehend and return him to the farm or that Jacob would recruit him for service in the Confederate army.

According to NARA documents, after Parson completed military service, he returned to Southampton County and assumed the surname of Sykes. Besides verifying his alias surname, in the documents recorded various given names. On November 10, 1899, Henry Charity supplied an affidavit on Parson's behalf, attesting that he knew Parson all his life, and Harrison Williams was an alias. Henry Charity and Parson joined the Union Army at the same time and place. They left the army at the same time and returned home together and lived in the same County. According to documents included the

NARA, Civil War pension collection, Parson Sykes married Frances Hill on March 18, 1867. They were married for over thirty years and lived together as spouses until his death. Parson and Frances had fourteen children: John, Frank, Annie, Eddie, Mattie, Mary, Freddie, Joseph, Hattie, James, Hubbard, Paul, Waverley, and Willie. According to Jacob's daughter, Parthenia Williams, Parson, and Frances lived on her property until they had several children.

After completing military service, Joseph Sykes, alias Joseph Williams, returned to Southampton County. He married Margaret Jane Whitehead on December 14, 1876. He lived with her until his death in December 1897. They had three children, Virginia, Lue Nettie, and Cora Bell Williams or (Sykes). According to NARA documents, Jacob's grandson, F. E. Williams, attested on December 20, 1898, that he had been acquainted with Joseph Sykes or Williams all his life and that Joseph was a slave of his grandfather Jacob Williams. As was the custom, according to F. E. Williams, he was known by the name of Joseph Williams, but after liberation, he assumed the surname of his father, who was Solomon Sykes. After serving honorably in the Army, Henry Sykes returned to Southampton County. He married Margaret Harrison under the slave law. They had two children together, Louis born on December 28, 1876: Maggie born May 4, 1878. After Margaret died on June 11, 1884, in Southampton County, Henry married Harriett Madison on April 18, 1877, in Southampton County, Virginia. Harriett's parents were Giles and Arsenia Madison.

Solomon and Louisa continued enslavement on Jacob's farm until the conclusion of the Civil War and the Union victory. Racism and discrimination continued to permeate all aspects of Black people's lives because of the unchecked existence of and the emergence of white supremacy groups that attempted to keep Black people within restricted social, economic, and political boundaries.

Jacob Williams showed no inclination to change his ways and views. He kept his racist, white supremacy values and the politics that characterized him before and after the Civil War. To Jacob, the social status quo was the same as the law. He still felt Black people were more violent and dangerous, not disturbed by harsh labor, physical brutality, and not fully human. Through sharecropping and tenant-farming, he gained advantage from institutional racism and promoted racist ideas that boosted him in status above poor white and Black people. Once Parson and his brothers returned to Southampton County, they were local heroes for the important part they played in winning freedom for their race. With the pay and enlistment bounties, they could buy land, set up commercial farms, and assume leadership roles in the Black community. While the brothers advanced from their time in the Union Army, when they returned to Southampton County, local whites made them feel unwelcome. They and their families endured harassment, physical abuse, and economic discrimination.

From Contraband to USCT Regiments

Behavior like Jacob's toward Black people and ambitions to continue the Confederacy forced the question of slavery to the top of Union war issues. Parson refused to cooperate, escaped from enslavement, served honorably in the historic USCT Regiments of the Union Army. Most Americans are now familiar with a few of the subordinate units assigned to the regiments such as 54th and 55th Massachusetts regiments. Less well known is the role of the XXV Corps, a consolidation of thirty-two regiments of infantry and one of cavalry, played during the American Civil War. Parson spent his entire enlistment with the XXV Corps of the Union Army of the James. Most northern soldiers went to war to preserve the Union, but the war ultimately transformed into a struggle to eradicate slavery. Black people, both enslaved and free, pressed emancipation and nurtured this transformation. While Lincoln, his cabinet, and the War Department devised strategies to defeat the rebel insurrection, Black Americans quickly forced slavery as a primary issue in the debate.

Enslaved Black people who took freedom into their own hands and ran to Union lines congregated in contraband camps, which existed alongside Union Army camps. Fugitives posed a dilemma for the Union military. Army regulations prohibited soldiers from interfering with slavery or helping runaways, but many soldiers found such a policy unchristian. In May 1861, General Benjamin F. Butler exceeded his authority and began accepting freedom-seeking escapees who came to Fort Monroe in Virginia. He called them "contraband of war," and argued he had as much a right to seize them as he did to seize enemy weapons. Later, in 1861, Congress affirmed Butler's policy in the First Confiscation Act.

Life as contraband offered a potential path to freedom, and thousands of enslaved people seized the opportunity. Following the First Confiscation Act, in April 1862, Congress abolished the institution of slavery in the District of Columbia. In July 1862, Congress passed the Second Confiscation Act (Militia Act of 1862), making it legal for African American men to enlist in the United States Army "to construct entrenchments, or performing camp service or any other labor, or any military or naval service for which they may be found competent." The law also offered emancipation to any enslaved person willing and able to serve and their families, with the stipulation that their owner be disloyal to the Union.

In a few acts of congress, thousands of enslaved people went from contraband of war to comrade-in-arms. Word traveled fast among enslaved people, and this legislation led to even more runaways making their way into Union lines. Abraham Lincoln's thinking developed. During the summer of 1862, Lincoln first revealed his vision of emancipation to members of his cabinet.

In August 1862, Lincoln proposed his first iteration of the Emancipation Proclamation. It was not in its terms and conditions a full end to slavery; however, it shifted the crisis from a war for union to a war for emancipation. Lincoln's proclamation read that such persons of suitable condition to enter the armed service of the United States to garrison forts, positions, stations, and other place, and to serve on vessels of all sorts in said service. When the Emancipation Proclamation went into effect on January 1, 1863, widespread black enlistment ensued.

Later, May 22, 1863, the War Department issued General Order 143, creating the United States Colored Troops. The creation of United States Colored Troops regiments was a novel innovation during the Civil War. Northern free Black men and newly freed men joined under the leadership of white officers to fight for the Union cause. This novelty was not only beneficial for the Union war effort; it also showed the Confederacy that the Union aimed to destroy the status quo upon which their nation thrived. As Union armies penetrated deeper into the Confederacy, politicians and generals came to understand the necessity and benefit of enlisting Black men in the army.

The presence of Parson, Joseph, and Henry as armed, blue-clad soldiers sent shock waves throughout Jacob's mind and body. Parson and other Black soldiers defied the inequality of military service and used their positions in the army to reshape the social, political, and economic customs in the North and South. To their parents and families, they symbolized the embodiment of liberation and the end of slavery. To Jacob, they depicted the utter disruption of slavery and white supremacy that made up the cornerstone of the Confederate States of America.

As documented governmental records, throughout the war to preserve the Union, the military used thousands of Black refugees as servants, teamsters, laborers, cooks, and in other support duties. These types of duties did not qualify them as soldiers. Some of these men may have joined the USCT regiments later in the war for emancipation. Most of the USCT regiments occupied the Confederacy and performed admirably on the battlefield, shattering white myths that docile, cowardly Black men would fold in the turmoil of war. Black troops fought in over four hundred battles and skirmishes.

General Butler's Contraband of War decision changed the very purpose of the war, transforming it from a War Between the States into a conflict defending the United States' concept of freedom. Despite Union success in the summer of 1863, discontent over the war simmered across the North. This was true in the wake of the Enrollment Act—the first effort at a draft among the northern populace during the Civil War. Working-class northerners were especially angry that the wealthy could pay $300 for substitutes, sparing themselves from the carnage of war. In northern newspapers, "A rich man's war, but a poor man's fight," was a popular refrain. By the spring of 1865, the actions of Black troops were pushing the Union toward a victorious end to the War of emancipation.

Army of the James (USA) Reorganization

On December 3, 1864, the United States War Department issued General Order No. 297 reorganizing the Army of the James. The order discontinued the Army X Corps, and XVIII Corps. Officials merged the white infantry troops from the two corps to form the new XXIV Army Corps commanded by Major General Edward Ord. They melded Black regiments from the two discontinued corps to create the new Army XXV Corps commanded by Major General Godfrey Weitzel. Later in December, Grant ordered Butler to lead a provisional corps of his army in an assault on Fort Fisher, which guarded the port of Wilmington, North Carolina, the Confederacy's last major Atlantic seaport. Operating with Rear Admiral David D. Porter, Butler troops began landing near the fort following a naval bombardment of over 10,000 shells. After establishing a beachhead, Butler incurred Grant's wrath when he called off the operation after deciding that the shelling had not damaged the fort enough to capture it.

On January 7, 1865, the Adjutant General's Office issued General Order Number 1, which stated in part that, "By direction of the President of the United States, Major General Benjamin F. Butler is relieved from the command of the Department of North Carolina and Virginia." On the same day, United States Army Headquarters issued special orders appointing Major General Edward Ord to temporary command of the Department and of the Army of the James.

The Union forces returned to Fort Fisher on January 13, this time under Major General Alfred Terry. Lieutenant General Ulysses S. Grant chose him to lead a Provisional Corps of 9,000 troops from the Army of the James. According to historical military records, Rear Admiral David D. Porter returned with almost sixty vessels of the North Atlantic Blockading Squadron to the North Carolina coast after the failed December attempt.

One division of U.S. Colored Troops under Brig. Gen. Charles J. Paine would attack Maj. Gen. Robert Hoke's infantry line north of the fort, and a second division under Brig. Gen. Adelbert Ames, along with Porter's Marines and some sailors, would attack the earth and sand walls of the fort itself. Terry's infantry landed unopposed on January 13th, and two days later, after a naval bombardment, Union forces attacked. Maj. Gen. Hoke put up little resistance, so Paine's men joined Ames' brigades. After heavy fighting, Ames eventually gained the inside of the fort, and the Navy's heavy guns silenced the Confederate batteries. The garrison of the Confederate known as the "Gibraltar of the South" surrendered late that evening, opening the way for a Federal thrust against Wilmington.

Maj. Gen. Ord commanded the Army of the James throughout the rest of the Petersburg Campaign and during the Appomattox Campaign. When Richmond, Virginia fell on April 2, 1865, Parson, and the Black soldiers of the XXV Corps of the Army of the James were among the first Union troops to occupy the city. At Appomattox, the XXV Corps of the Army of the James cut off the Army of Northern Virginia's last avenue of escape, prompting Robert E. Lee's Army of Northern Virginia to surrender.

Contributions To Union Victory

Throughout the war, some of Jacob's neighbors suggested the Confederacy enlist Black men, which their government flatly rejected. Late in the war, as Confederate ranks dwindled, calls for the enlistment of Black men grew louder. Given such overwhelming military and public opinion and realizing the desperateness of their situation, the Confederate Congress passed an act allowing the enlistment of slaves into the Army. Each state was to enroll 300,000 slaves but, the act lacked the emancipation for volunteers. When the war ended in the year 1865, however, the Confederacy was organizing its first black units in Richmond.

Shortly after it fell, and the Confederate surrendered, Major Martin Delany, the first black field grade officer in the Union Army, announced, that if it were not for the Black men, the Civil War never would have ended with for success to the Union, and liberty for Black people. These words sound bold, even overblown, but his statement differed little from Abraham Lincoln's own assessment. By the war's end, almost 37,000 Black soldiers gave their lives to the restoration of the Union and the destruction of slavery.

Saddest of all, though, with the passing of each decade, the white population forgot increasingly about black military service in the war. Many of the black units remained on active service long after Appomattox, performing occupation duty in the Southern states and serving in the West. The USCT units would survive until December 1867, when the War Department replaced them with four regular Army regiments — 24th and 25th Infantry Regiments and 9th and 10th Cavalry Regiments. By the time of the First World War, Black Americans had to fight all the same racism that their antebellum ancestors fought centuries before.

Emancipation and the End of Legal Slavery

Before they could enlist, Black people passed through a series of phases of increasing levels of human rights. From enslavement, they went to refugee camps and labeled as contraband of war. Next, many Black people volunteered their services to the Union Army as cooks, nurses, and teamsters in other informal roles. States raised several Volunteer regiments of Black troops without federal authorization and recognition. Finally, after emancipation, the Union Army highly recruited Black men for USCT regiments to meet human resources requirements in the Union Army.

Emancipation and the end of legal slavery did not mean the end of racial injustice. During the war, the Union Army often segregated formerly enslaved people into disease-ridden contraband camps. Long after 1865, most Black southerners continued to labor on plantations, although as nominally free tenants or sharecroppers, while facing public segregation and voting discrimination. The effects of slavery endured long after emancipation.

Over the last 75 years, most Parson Sykes descendants' reunions were in Southampton County, Virginia. The family reunions usually included plenty of local grown food, historic speeches, and a guided tour tracing the path of the Nat Turner rebellion. These events preserve Parson's legacy of resisting enslavement and overcoming racial discrimination, uplift through self-determination. The reunions continue to stabilize the Sykes family as it struggles to survive today amid rapidly changing and increasingly complex political, economic, and social conditions.

The next volume will describe historic encounters by Parson during his enlistment at City Point and in Richmond. In April 1865, he went with General Weitzel to Richmond, as his all Black XXV Corps entered the city first. In May 1865, Parson went with the XXV Corps to Texas, where it joined the Army of Occupation, and remained until January 8, 1866.

THE END

About the Author

 COL David J. Mason, U.S. Army, Retired, is Owner and Founder of HMG ePublishing, LLC, and the great grandson of Parson Sykes.

He is an online entrepreneur, author, digital publisher, and veteran senior executive, who has been on the Internet since 1997 He has executive experience leading, administering and directing scientific, technological, and military operations for a wide range of organization including government, academic, private industry, trade associations, and the public.

Mr. Mason became interested in the history of the Sykes family early in life while attending family reunions and hearing stories of his mother's ancestors from Southampton County, Virginia. The family descended from Louisa Williams Sykes, an enslaved African American matriarch who had lived on Jacob Williams' farm on Barrow Road in the Cross Keys neighborhood. During the 1831 Southampton Insurrection, the farm came under attack by Nat Turner and his insurgents.

For over 150 years, Parson Sykes' descendants passed down stories and adventures of Parson's early life at family reunions and holiday meals, weddings, and other gatherings where the ancestors met. During Civil War, Parson and his brothers, Joseph, and Henry made a challenging escape from bondage to reach Fort Monroe in early December 1864 and, after enlistment, they performed successful combat military duty with the 25th Army Corps United States Colored Troops (USCT).

Intrigued by what he heard at family gathering, David researched Parson, Joseph, and Henry military service and published The *Self-Liberation of Parson Sykes* a documentary novel based on the true self-liberation ordeal and actual events drawn from a variety of sources, including published materials and family chronicles. In the book, Parson and Jacob Williams are faced at opposite ends of the disputed points over the moral issue of slavery and secession, a political decision that led directly to war. The novel profiles Parson's evolution from enslavement and self-liberation by running away from Jacob Williams' farm.

The sequel to this documentary novel based on Parson's military service with Company I, First Cavalry Regimental USCT of the Union Army XXV Corps, will follow this novel. On April 3, 1865, units of the Army XXV Corps were among the first to enter the city that for the past four years been the capital of the Confederacy, where Parson arrives at his destination. At the conclusion of the Civil War, the army ordered the XXV Corps to Texas for border duty.

Mr. Mason is author of Environmental Compliance Tool Kit (Thompson Publishing Group, 1994) and the Internet Marketing Tool Kit (HMG ePublishing, 2006). He holds a Master of Science degree in chemistry from Hampton University in Virginia, a Bachelor of Science degree in chemistry from Norfolk State University and is a graduate of the Army War College.

Appendices

This novel has the following six appendices depicting the historical documents referred to or mentioned in it.

Appendix A: The Fugitive Slave Act of 1793

An Act respecting fugitives from justice, and persons escaping from the service of their masters.

Appendix B: The Fugitive Slave Act of 1850

An Act to amend, and supplementary to, the Act entitled "An Act respecting Fugitives from Justice, and Persons escaping from the Service of their Masters," approved February twelfth, one thousand seven hundred and ninety-three.

Appendix C: The Confiscation Act

An Act to confiscate Property used for insurrectionary purposes.

Appendix D: The Militia Act, July 17, 1862

An Act to amend the Act calling forth the Militia to execute the Laws of the Union, suppress Insurrections, and repel Invasion, approved February twenty-eight, seventeen hundred and ninety-five, and the Acts amendatory thereof, and for other purposes.

Appendix E: The Emancipation Proclamation

A proclamation issued by the President of the United States that on the twenty-second day of September, in one thousand eight hundred and sixty-two, all persons held as slaves within any State or designated part of a State, the people whereof shall then be in rebellion against the United States, shall be then, *"thence forward, and forever free, among other things."*

Appendix F: The Conscription Act, 1863

An Act for enrolling and calling out the national Forces, and for other purposes.

Appendix A

The Fugitive Slave Act of 1793

February 12, 1793

Statutes at Large, Chap. VII, p. 302, February 12, 1793, Chapter VIIC.

An Act respecting fugitives from justice, and persons escaping from the service of their masters.

Section 1. Be it enacted by the Senate and House of Representatives of the United States of America in Congress assembled, That whenever the executive authority of any state in the Union, or of either of the territories northwest or south of the river Ohio, shall demand any person as a fugitive from justice, of the executive authority of any such state or territory to which such person shall have fled, and shall moreover produce the copy of an indictment found, or an affidavit made before a magistrate of any state or territory as aforesaid, charging the person so demanded, with having committed treason, felony or other crime, certified as authentic by the governor or chief magistrate of the state or territory from whence the person so charged fled, it shall be the duty of the executive authority of the state or territory to which such person shall have fled, to cause him or her to be arrested and secured, and notice of the arrest to be given to the executive authority making such demand, or to the agent of such authority appointed to receive the fugitive, and to cause the fugitive to be delivered to such agent when he shall appear: But if no such agent shall appear within six months from the time of the arrest, the prisoner may be discharged. And all costs or expenses incurred in the apprehending, securing, and transmitting such fugitive to the state or territory making such demand, shall be paid by such state or territory.

Section 2. And be it further enacted, That any agent, appointed as aforesaid, who shall receive the fugitive into his custody, shall be empowered to transport him or her to the state or territory from which he or she shall have fled. And if any person or persons shall by force set at liberty, or rescue the fugitive from such agent while transporting, as aforesaid, the person or persons so offending shall, on conviction, be fined not exceeding five hundred dollars, and be imprisoned not exceeding one year.

Section 3. And it be also enacted, That when a person held to labor in any of the United States, or in either of the territories on the northwest or south of the river Ohio, under the laws thereof, shall escape into any other of the said states or territory, the person to whom such labor or service may be due, his agent or attorney, is hereby empowered to seize or arrest such fugitive from labor, (b) and to take him or her before any judge of the circuit or district courts of the United States, residing or being within the state, or being any magistrate of a county, city or town corporate, wherein such seizure or arrest shall be made, and upon proof to the satisfaction of such judge or magistrate, either by oral testimony or affidavit taken before and certified by a magistrate of any such state or territory, that the person so seized or arrested, doth, under the laws of the state or territory from which he or she fled, owe service or labor to the person claiming him or her, it shall be the duty of such judge or magistrate to give a certificate thereof to such claimant, his agent or attorney, which shall be sufficient warrant for removing the said fugitive from labor, to the state or territory from which he or she fled.

Section 4. And it be further enacted, That any person who shall knowingly and willingly obstruct or hinder such claimant, his agent or attorney in so seizing or arresting such fugitive from labor, or shall rescue such fugitive from such claimant, his agent or attorney when so arrested pursuant to the authority herein given or declared; or shall harbor or conceal such person after notice that he or she was a fugitive from labor, as aforesaid, shall for either of the said offences, forfeit and pay the sum of five hundred dollars. Which penalty may be recovered by and for the benefit of such claimant, by the action of debt, in any court proper to try the same, saving moreover to the person claiming such labor or service, his right of action for or on account of the said injuries or either of them.

APPROVED, February 12, 1793

Appendix B

The Fugitive Slave Act of 1850

September 18, 1850

An Act to amend, and supplementary to, the Act entitled "An Act respecting Fugitives from Justice, and Persons escaping from the Service of their Masters," approved February twelfth, one thousand seven hundred and ninety-three.

Be it enacted by the Senate and House of Representatives of the United States of America in congress assembled, That the persons who have been, or may hereafter be, appointed commissioners, in virtue of any act of Congress, by the Circuit Courts of the United States and who, in consequence of such appointment, are authorized to exercise the powers that any justice of the peace, or other magistrate of any of the United States, may exercise in respect to offenders for any crime or offence against the United States, by arresting, imprisoning, or bailing the same under and by virtue of the thirty-third section of the act of the twenty-fourth of September seventeen hundred and eighty-nine, entitled " An Act to establish the Judicial courts of the United States," shall be, and are hereby, authorized and required to exercise and discharge all the powers and duties conferred by this act.

SEC. 2. And be it further enacted, That the Superior Court of each organized Territory of the United States shall have the same power to appoint commissioners to take acknowledgements of bail and affidavits and to take depositions of witnesses in civil causes, which is now possessed by the Circuit Court of the United States; and all commissioners who shall hereafter be appointed for such purposes by the Superior Court of any organized Territory of the United States, shall possess all the powers, and exercise all the duties, conferred by law upon the commissioners appointed by the Circuit Courts of the United States for similar purposes, and shall moreover exercise and discharge all the powers and duties conferred by this act.

SEC. 3. And be it further enacted, That the Circuit Courts of the United States, and the Superior Courts of each organized Territory of the United States, shall from time to time enlarge the number of commissioners, with a view to afford reasonable facilities to reclaim fugitives from labor, and to the prompt discharge of the duties imposed by this act.

SEC. 4. And be it further enacted, That the commissioners above named shall have concurrent jurisdiction with the judges of the Circuit and District Courts of the United States, in their respective circuits and districts within the several States, and the judges of the Superior Courts of the Territories, severally and collectively, in term- time and vacation; and shall grant certificates to such claimants, upon satisfactory proof being made, with authority to take and remove such fugitives from service or labor, under the restrictions herein contained, to the State or Territory from which such persons may have escaped or fled.

SEC. 5. And be it further enacted, That it shall be the duty of all marshals and deputy marshals to obey and execute all warrants and precepts issued under the provisions of this act, when to them directed ; and should any marshal or deputy marshal refuse to receive such warrant, or other process, when tendered, or to use all proper means diligently to execute the same, he shall, on conviction thereof, be fined in the sum of one thousand dollars, to the use of such claimant, on the motion of such claimant, by the Circuit or District Court for the district of such marshal;

and after arrest of such fugitive, by such marshal or his deputy, or whilst at any time in his custody under the provisions of this act, should such fugitive escape, whether with or without the assent of such marshal or his deputy, such marshal shall be liable, on his official bond, to be prosecuted for the benefit of such claimant, for the full value of the service or labor of said fugitive in the State, Territory, or District whence he escaped: and the better to enable the said commissioners, when thus appointed, to execute their duties faithfully and efficiently, in conformity with the requirements of the Constitution of the United States and of this act, they are hereby authorized and empowered, within their counties respectively, to appoint, in writing under their hands, anyone or more suitable persons, from time to time, to execute all such warrants and other process as may be issued by them in the lawful performance of their respective duties; with authority to such commissioners, or the persons to be appointed by them, to execute process as aforesaid, to summon and call to their aid the bystanders, or posse comitatus of the proper county, when necessary to ensure a faithful observance of the clause of the Constitution referred to, in conformity with the provisions of this act ; and all good citizens are hereby commanded to aid and assist in the prompt and efficient execution of this law, whenever their services may he required, as aforesaid, for that purpose; and said warrants shall run, and be executed by said officers, any where in the State within which they are issued.

SEC. 6. And be it further enacted, That when a person held to service or labor in any State or Territory of the United States, has heretofore or shall hereafter escape into another State or Territory of the United States, the person or persons to whom such service or labor may be due, or his, her, or their agent or attorney, duly authorized, by power of attorney, in writing, acknowledged and certified under the seal of some legal officer or court of the State or Territory in which the same may be executed, may pursue and reclaim such fugitive person, either by procuring a warrant from some one of the courts, judges, or commissioners aforesaid, of the proper circuit, district, or county, for the apprehension of such fugitive from service or labor, or by seizing and arresting such fugitive, where the same can be done without process, and by taking, or causing such person to be taken, forthwith before such court, judge, or commissioner, whose duty it shall be to hear and determine the case of such claimant in a summary manner; and upon satisfactory proof being made, by deposition or affidavit, in writing, to be taken and certified by such court, judge, or commissioner, or by other satisfactory testimony, duly taken and certified by some court, magistrate, justice of the peace, or other legal officer authorized to administer an oath and take depositions under the laws of the State or Territory from which such person owing service or labor may have escaped, with a certificate of such magistracy or other authority, as aforesaid, with the seal of the proper court or officer thereto attached, which seal shall be sufficient to establish the competency of the proof, and with proof, also by affidavit, of the identity of the person whose service or labor is claimed to be due as aforesaid, that the person so arrested does in fact owe service or labor to the person or persons claiming him or her, in the State or Territory from which such fugitive may have escaped as aforesaid, and that said person escaped, to make out and deliver to such claimant, his or her agent or attorney, a certificate setting forth the substantial facts as to the service or labor due from such fugitive to the claimant, and of his or her escape from the State or Territory in which such service or labor was due, to the State or Territory in which he or she was arrested, with authority to such claimant, or his or her agent or attorney, to use such reasonable force and restraint as may be necessary, under the circumstances of the case, to take and remove such fugitive person back to the State or Territory whence he or she may have escaped as aforesaid. In no trial or hearing under this act shall the testimony of such alleged fugitive be admitted in evidence; and the certificates in this and the first [fourth] section mentioned, shall be conclusive of the right of the person or persons in whose favor granted, to remove such fugitive to the State or Territory from which he escaped, and shall prevent all molestation of such person or persons by any process issued by any court judge, magistrate, or other person whomsoever.

SEC. 7. And be it further enacted, That any person who shall knowingly and willingly obstruct, hinder, or prevent such claimant, his agent or attorney, or any person or persons lawfully assisting him, her, or them, from arresting such a fugitive from service or labor, either with or without process as aforesaid, or shall rescue, or attempt to rescue such fugitive from service or labor, from the custody of such claimant, his or her agent or attorney, or other person or persons lawfully assisting as aforesaid, when so arrested, pursuant to the authority herein given and declared; or shall aid, abet, or assist such person so owing service or labor as aforesaid, directly or indirectly, to escape from such claimant, his agent or attorney, or other person or persons legally authorized as aforesaid; or shall harbor or conceal such fugitive, so as to prevent the discovery and arrest of such person, after notice or knowledge of the fact that such person was a fugitive from service or labor as aforesaid, shall, for either of said offences, be subject to a fine not exceeding one thousand dollars, and imprisonment not exceeding six months, by indictment and conviction before the District Court of the United States for the district in which such offence may have been committed, or before the proper court of criminal jurisdiction, if committed within anyone of the organized Territories of the United States; and shall moreover forfeit and pay, by way of civil damages to the party injured by such illegal conduct, the sum of one thousand dollars, for each fugitive so lost as aforesaid, to be recovered by action of debt, in any of the District or Territorial Courts aforesaid, within whose jurisdiction the said offence may have been committed.

SEC. 8. And be it further enacted, That the marshals, their deputies, and the clerks of the said District and Territorial Courts, shall be paid, for their services, the like fees as may be allowed to them for similar services in other cases; and where such services are rendered exclusively in the arrest, custody, and delivery of the fugitive to the claimant, his or her agent or attorney, or where such supposed fugitive may be discharged out of custody for the want of sufficient proof as aforesaid, then such fees are to be paid in the whole by such claimant, his agent or attorney; and in all cases where the proceedings are before a commissioner, he shall be entitled to a fee of ten dollars in full for his services in each case, upon the delivery of the said certificate to the claimant, his or her agent or attorney; or a fee of five dollars in cases where the proof shall not, in the opinion of such commissioner, war- rant such certificate and delivery, inclusive of all services incident to such arrest and examination, to be paid, in either case, by the claimant, his or her agent or attorney The person or persons authorized to exe- cute the process to be issued by such commissioners for the arrest and detention of fugitives from service or labor as aforesaid, shall also be entitled to a fee of five dollars each for each person he or they may arrest and take before any such commissioner as aforesaid, at the instance and request of such claimant, with such other fees as may be deemed reasonable by such commissioner for such other additional services as may be necessarily performed by him or them; such as attending at the examination, keeping the fugitive in custody, and providing him with food and lodging during his detention, and until the final determination of such commissioner; and, in general, for performing such other duties as may be required by such claimant, his or her attorney or agent, or commissioner in the premises, such fees to be made up in conformity with the fees usually charged by the officers of the courts of justice within the proper district or county, as near as may be practicable, and paid by such claimants, their agents or attorneys, whether such supposed fugitives from service or labor be ordered to be delivered to such claimants by the final determination of such commissioners or not.

SEC. 9. And be it further enacted, That, upon affidavit made by the claimant of such fugitive, his agent or attorney, after such certificate has been issued, that he has reason to apprehend that such fugitive will be rescued by force from his or their possession before he can be taken beyond the limits of the State in which the arrest is made, it shall be the duty of the officer making the arrest to retain such fugitive in his custody, and to remove him to the State whence he fled, and there to deliver him to said claimant, his agent, or attorney. And to this end, the officer aforesaid is hereby authorized and required to employ so many persons as he may deem necessary to overcome such force, and to retain them in his service so long as circumstances may require. The said officer and his assistants, while so employed, to receive the same compensation, and to be allowed the same expenses, as are now allowed by law for transportation of criminals, to be certified by the judge of the district within which the arrest is made and paid out of the treasury of the United States.

SEC. 10. And be it further enacted, That when any person held to service or labor in any State or Territory, or in the District of Columbia, shall escape therefrom, the party to whom such service or labor shall be due, his, her, or their agent or attorney, may apply to any court of record therein, or judge thereof in vacation, and make satisfactory proof to such court, or judge in vacation, of the escape aforesaid, and that the person escaping owed service or labor to such party. Whereupon the court shall cause a record to be made of the matters so proved, and also a general description of the person so escaping, with such convenient certainty as may be; and a transcript of such record, authenticated by the attestation of the clerk and of the seal of the said court, being produced in any other State, Territory, or district in which the person so escaping may be found, and being exhibited to any judge, commissioner, or other officer authorized by the law of the United States to cause persons escaping from service or labor to be delivered up, shall be held and taken to be full and conclusive evidence of the fact of escape, and that the service or labor of the person escaping is due to the party in such record mentioned. And upon the production by the said party of the other and further evidence, if necessary, either oral or by affidavit, in addition to what is contained in the said record of the identity of the person escaping, he or she shall be delivered up to the claimant. And the said court, commissioner, judge, or other person authorized by this act to grant certificates to claimants of fugitives, shall, upon the production of the record and other evidences aforesaid, grant to such claimant a certificate of his right to take any such person identified and proved to be owing service or labor as aforesaid, which certificate shall authorize such claimant to seize or arrest and transport such person to the State or Territory from which he escaped: Provided, That nothing herein contained shall be construed as requiring the production of a transcript of such record as evidence as aforesaid. But in its absence the claim shall be heard and determined upon other satisfactory proofs, competent in law.

APPROVED, September 18, 1850

Appendix C

The Confiscation Act

August 6, 1861

CHAP. LX. –An Act to confiscate Property used for Insurrectionary Purposes.

Be it enacted by the Senate and House of Representatives of the United States of America in Congress assembled, That if, during the present or any future insurrection against the Government of the United States, after the President of the United States shall have declared, by proclamation, that the laws of the United States are opposed, and the execution thereof obstructed, by combinations too powerful to be suppressed by the ordinary course of judicial proceedings, or by the power vested in the marshals by law, any person or persons, his, her, or their agent, attorney, or employee, shall purchase or acquire, sell or give, any property of whatsoever kind or description, with intent to use or employ the same, or suffer the same to be used or employed, in aiding, abetting, or promoting such insurrection or resistance to the laws, or any person or persons engaged therein; or if any person or persons, being the owner or owners of any such property, shall knowingly use or employ, or consent to the use or employment of the same as aforesaid, all such property is hereby declared to be lawful subject of prize and capture wherever found; and it shall be the duty of the President of the United States to cause the same to be seized, confiscated, and condemned.

SEC. 2. And be it further enacted, That such prizes and capture shall be condemned in the district or circuit court of the United States having jurisdiction of the amount, or in admiralty in any district in which the same may be seized, or into which they may be taken and proceedings first instituted.

SEC. 3. And be it further enacted, That the Attorney-General, or any district attorney of the United States in which said property may at the time be, may institute the proceedings of condemnation, and in such case they shall be wholly for the benefit of the United States; or any person may file an information with such attorney, in which case the proceedings shall be for the use of such informer and the United States in equal parts.

SEC. 4. And be it further enacted, That whenever hereafter, during the present insurrection against the Government of the United States, any person claimed to be held to labor or service under the law of any State, shall be required or permitted by the person to whom such labor or service is claimed to be due, or by the lawful agent of such person, to take up arms against the United States, or shall be required or permitted by the person to whom such labor or service is claimed to be due, or his lawful agent, to work or to be employed in or upon any fort, navy yard, dock, armory, ship, entrenchment, or in any military or naval service whatsoever, against the Government and lawful authority of the United States, then, and in every such case, the person to whom such labor or service is claimed to be due shall forfeit his claim to such labor, any law of the State or of the United States to the contrary notwithstanding. And whenever thereafter the person claiming such labor or service shall seek to enforce his claim, it shall be a full and sufficient answer to such claim that the person whose service or labor is claimed had been employed in hostile service against the Government of the United States, contrary to the provisions of this act.

APPROVED, August 6, 186

Appendix D
The Militia Act 1862

July 17, 1862

CHAP. CCI. – An Act to amend the Act calling forth the Militia to execute the Laws of the Union, suppress Insurrections, and repel Invasion, approved February twenty-eight, seventeen hundred and ninety-five, and the Acts amendatory thereof, and for other Purposes.

SEC. 2. And be it further enacted, That the militia, when so called into service, shall be organized in the mode prescribed by law for volunteers.

SEC. 3. And be it further enacted, That the President be, and he is hereby, authorized, in addition to the volunteer forces which he is now authorized by law to raise, to accept the services of any number of volunteers, not exceeding one hundred thousand, as infantry, for a period of nine months, unless sooner discharged. And every soldier who shall enlist under the provisions of this section shall receive his first month's pay, and also twenty-five dollars as bounty, upon the mustering of his company or regiment into the service of the United States. And all provisions of law relating to volunteers enlisted in the service of the United States for three years, or during the war, except in relation to bounty, shall be, and the same are, extended to, and are hereby declared to embrace, the volunteers to be raised under the provisions of this section.

SEC. 4. And be it further enacted, That, for the purpose of filling up the regiments of infantry now in the United States service, the President be, and he hereby is, authorized to accept the services of volunteers in such numbers as may be presented for that purpose, for twelve months, if not sooner discharged. And such volunteers, when mustered into the service, shall be in all respects upon a footing with similar troops in the United States service, except as to service bounty, which shall be fifty dollars, one half of which to be paid upon their joining their regiments, and the other half at the expiration of their enlistment.

SEC. 5. And be it further enacted, That the President shall appoint, by and with the advice and consent of the Senate, a judge advocate general, with the rank, pay, and emoluments of a colonel of cavalry, to whose office shall be returned, for revision, the records and proceedings of all courts martial and military commissions, and where a record shall be kept of all proceedings had thereupon. And no sentence of death, or imprisonment in the penitentiary, shall be carried into execution until the same shall have been approved by the President.

SEC. 6. And be it further enacted, That there may be appointed by the President, by and with the advice and consent of the Senate, for each army in the field, a judge advocate, with the rank, pay, and emoluments, each, of a major cavalry, who shall perform the duties of judge advocate for the army to which they respectively belong, under the direction of the judge advocate general.

SEC. 7. And be it further enacted, That hereafter all offenders in the army charged with offences now punishable by a regimental or garrison court-martial, shall be brought before a field officer of his regiment, who shall be detailed for that purpose, and who shall hear and determine the offence, and order the punishment that shall be inflicted; and shall also make a record of his proceedings, and submit the same to the brigade commander, who, upon the approval of the proceedings of such field officer, shall order the same to be executed: Provided, That the punishment in such cases be limited to that authorized to be inflicted by a regimental or garrison court-martial: And provided, further, That, in the event of there being no brigade commander, the proceedings as aforesaid shall be submitted for approval to the commanding officer of the post.

SEC. 8. And be it further enacted, That all officers who have been mustered into the service of the United States as battalion adjutants and quartermasters of cavalry under the orders of the War Department, exceeding the number authorized by law, shall be paid as such for the time the service they were actually employed in the service of the United States, and that all such officers now in service, exceeding the number as aforesaid, shall be immediately mustered out of the service of the United States.

SEC. 9. And be it further enacted, That the President be, and he is hereby authorized to establish and army corps according to his discretion.

SEC. 10. And be it further enacted, That each army corps shall have the following officers no more attached thereto, who shall constitute the staff of the commander thereof: one assistant adjutant general, one Staff quartermaster, one commissary of subsistence, and one assistant inspector general, who shall bear, respectively, the rank of lieutenant colonel, and who shall be assigned from the army or volunteer force by the President. Also, three aides-de-camp, one to bear the rank of major, and two to bear the rank of captain, to be appointed by the President, by and with the advice and consent of the Senate, upon the recommendation of the commander of the army corps. The senior officer of artillery in each army corps shall, in addition to his other duties, act as chief of artillery and ordnance at the headquarters of the corps.

SEC. 11. And be it further enacted, That the cavalry forces in the service of the United States shall hereafter be organized as follows: Each regiment of cavalry shall have one colonel, one lieutenant colonel, three majors, one surgeon, one assistant surgeon, one regimental adjutant, one regimental quartermaster, one regimental commissary, one sergeant major, one quartermaster sergeant, one commissary sergeant, two hospital stewards, one saddler sergeant, one chief trumpeter, and one chief farrier or blacksmith, and each regiment shall consist of twelve companies or troops, and each company or troop shall have one captain, one first lieutenant, one second lieutenant, and one supernumerary second lieutenant, one first sergeant, one quartermaster sergeant, one commissary sergeant, five sergeants, eight corporals, two teamsters, two farriers or blacksmiths, one saddler, one wagoner, and seventy-eight privates; the regimental adjutant, the regimental quartermasters, and regimental commissaries to be taken from their respective regiments: Provided, That vacancies caused by this organization shall not be considered as original, but shall be filled by regular promotion.

SEC. 12. And be it further enacted, That the President be, and he is hereby, authorized to receive into the service of the United States, for the purpose of constructing entrenchments, or performing camp service, or any other labor, or any military or naval service for which they may be found competent, persons of African descent, and such persons shall be enrolled and organized under such regulations, not inconsistent with the Constitution and laws, as the President may prescribe.

SEC. 13. And be it further enacted, That when any man or boy of African descent, who by the laws of any State shall owe service or labor to any person who, during the present rebellion, has levied war or has borne arms against the United States, or adhered to their enemies by giving them aid and comfort, shall render any such service as is provided for in this act, he, his mother and his wife and children, shall forever thereafter be free, any law, usage, or custom whatsoever to the contrary notwithstanding: Provided, That the mother, wife and children of such man or boy of African descent shall not be made free by the operation of this act except where such mother, wife or children owe service or labor to some person who, during the present rebellion, has borne arms against the United States or adhered to their enemies by giving them aid and comfort.

SEC. 14. And be it further enacted, That the expenses incurred to carry this act into effect shall be paid out of the general appropriation for the army and volunteers.

SEC. 15. And be it further enacted, That all persons who have been or shall be hereafter enrolled in the service of the United States under this act shall receive the pay and rations now allowed by law to soldiers, according to their respective grades: Provided, That persons of African Pay, &, of descent, who under this law shall be employed, shall receive ten dollars per month and one ration, three dollars of which monthly pay may be in clothing.

SEC. 16. And be it further enacted, That medical purveyors and storekeepers shall give bonds in such sums as the Secretary of War may require with security to be approved by him.

APPROVED, July 17, 1862

Appendix E
The Emancipation Proclamation

January 1, 1863

By the President of the United States of America:

A Proclamation.

Whereas, on the twenty-second day of September, in the year of our Lord one thousand eight hundred and sixty-two, a proclamation was issued by the President of the United States, containing, among other things, the following, to wit:

"That on the first day of January, in the year of our Lord one thousand eight hundred and sixty-three, all persons held as slaves within any State or designated part of a State, the people whereof shall then be in rebellion against the United States, shall be then, thenceforward, and forever free; and the Executive Government of the United States, including the military and naval authority thereof, will recognize and maintain the freedom of such persons, and will do no act or acts to repress such persons, or any of them, in any efforts they may make for their actual freedom.

"That the Executive will, on the first day of January aforesaid, by proclamation, designate the States and parts of States, if any, in which the people thereof, respectively, shall then be in rebellion against the United States; and the fact that any State, or the people thereof, shall on that day be, in good faith, represented in the Congress of the United States by members chosen thereto at elections wherein a majority of the qualified voters of such State shall have participated, shall, in the absence of strong countervailing testimony, be deemed conclusive evidence that such State, and the people thereof, are not then in rebellion against the United States."

Now, therefore I, Abraham Lincoln, President of the United States, by virtue of the power in me vested as Commander-in-Chief, of the Army and Navy of the United States in time of actual armed rebellion against the authority and government of the United States, and as a fit and necessary war measure for suppressing said rebellion, do, on this first day of January, in the year of our Lord one thousand eight hundred and sixty-three, and in accordance with my purpose so to do publicly proclaimed for the full period of one hundred days, from the day first above mentioned, order and designate as the States and parts of States wherein the people thereof respectively, are this day in rebellion against the United States, the following, to wit:

Arkansas, Texas, Louisiana, (except the Parishes of St. Bernard, Plaquemines, Jefferson, St. John, St. Charles, St. James Ascension, Assumption, Terrebonne, Lafourche, St. Mary, St. Martin, and Orleans, including the City of New Orleans) Mississippi, Alabama, Florida, Georgia, South Carolina, North Carolina, and Virginia, (except the forty-eight counties designated as West Virginia, and also the counties of Berkley, Accomac, Northampton, Elizabeth City, York, Princess Ann, and Norfolk, including the cities of Norfolk and Portsmouth), and which excepted parts, are for the present, left precisely as if this proclamation were not issued.

And by virtue of the power, and for the purpose aforesaid, I do order and declare that all persons held as slaves within said designated States, and parts of States, are, and henceforward shall be free; and that the Executive government of the United States, including the military and naval authorities thereof, will recognize and maintain the freedom of said persons.

And I hereby enjoin upon the people so declared to be free to abstain from all violence, unless in necessary self-defense; and I recommend to them that, in all cases when allowed, they labor faithfully for reasonable wages.

And I further declare and make known, that such persons of suitable condition, will be received into the armed service of the United States to garrison forts, positions, stations, and other places, and to man vessels of all sorts in said service.

And upon this act, sincerely believed to be an act of justice, warranted by the Constitution, upon military necessity, I invoke the considerate judgment of mankind, and the gracious favor of Almighty God. In witness whereof, I have hereunto set my hand and caused the seal of the United States to be affixed.

Done at the City of Washington, this first day of January, in the year of our Lord one thousand eight hundred and sixty-three, and of the Independence of the United States of America the eighty-seventh.

By the President: ABRAHAM LINCOLN

WILLIAM H. SEWARD, Secretary of State.

Appendix F
The Conscription Act, 1863

March 3, 1863

An Act for enrolling and calling out the national Forces, and for other Purposes.

Whereas there now exist in the United States an insurrection and rebellion against the authority thereof, and it is, under the Constitution of the United States, the duty of the government to suppress insurrection and rebellion, to guarantee to each State a republican form of government, and to preserve the public tranquility; and whereas, for these high purposes, a military force is indispensable, to raise and support which all persons ought willingly to contribute; and whereas no service can be more praiseworthy and honorable than that which is rendered for the maintenance of the Constitution and Union, and the consequent preservation of free government: Therefore -

Be it enacted by the Senate and House of Representatives of the United States of America in Congress assembled, That all able-bodied male citizens of the United States, and persons of foreign birth who shall have declared on oath their intention to become citizens under and in pursuance of the laws thereof, between the ages of twenty and forty-five years, except as hereinafter excepted, are hereby declared to constitute the national forces, and shall be liable to perform military duty in the service of the United States when called out by the President for that purpose.

SEC. 2. And be it further enacted, That the following persons be, and they are hereby, excepted and exempt from the provisions of this act, and shall not be liable to military duty under the same, to wit: Such as are rejected as physically or mentally unfit for the service; also, First the Vice-President of the United States, the judges of the various courts of the United States, the heads of the various executive departments of the government, and the governors of the several States. Second, the only son liable to military duty of a widow dependent upon his labor for support. Third, the only son of aged or infirm parent or parents dependent upon his labor for support. Fourth, where there are two or more sons of aged or infirm parents subject to draft, the father, or, if he is dead, the mother, may elect which son shall be exempt. Fifth, the only brother of children not twelve years old, having neither father nor mother dependent upon his labor for support. Sixth, the father of motherless children under twelve years of age dependent upon his labor for support. Seventh, where there are a father and sons in the same family and household, and two of them are in the military service of the United States as non-commissioned officers, musicians, or privates, the residue of such family and household, not exceeding two, shall be exempt. And no persons but such as are herein excepted shall be exempt: Provided, however, That no person who has been convicted of any felony shall be enrolled or permitted to serve in said forces.

SEC. 3. And be it further enacted, That the national forces of the United States not now in the military service, enrolled under this act, shall be pided into two classes: the first of which shall comprise all persons subject to do military duty between the ages of twenty and thirty-five years, and all unmarried persons subject to do military duty above the age of thirty-five and under the age of forty-five; the second class shall comprise all other persons subject to do military duty, and they shall not, in any district, be called into the service of the United States until those of the first class shall have been called.

SEC. 4. And be it further enacted, That, for greater convenience in enrolling, calling out, and organizing the national forces, and for the arrest of deserters and spies of the enemy, the United States shall be pided into districts, of which the District of Columbia shall constitute one, each territory of the United States shall constitute one or more, as the President shall direct, and each congressional district of the respective states, as fixed by a law of the state next preceding the enrolment, shall constitute one: Provided, That in states which have not by their laws been pided into two or more congressional districts, the President of the United States shall pide the same into so many enrolment districts as he may deem fit and convenient.

SEC. 5. And be it further enacted, That for each of said districts there shall be appointed by the President a provost-marshal, with the rank, pay, and emoluments of a captain of cavalry, or an officer of said rank shall be detailed by the President, who shall be under the direction and subject to the orders of a provost-marshal-general, appointed or detailed by the President of the United States, whose office shall be at the seat of government, forming a separate bureau of the War Department, and whose rank, pay, and emoluments shall be those of a colonel of cavalry.

SEC. 6. And be it further enacted, That it shall be the duty of the provost-marshal-general, with the approval of the Secretary of War, to make rules and regulations for the government of his subordinates; to furnish them with the names and residences of all deserters from the army, or any of the land forces in the service of the United States, including the militia, when reported to him by the commanding officers; to communicate to them all orders of the President in reference to calling out the national forces; to furnish proper blanks and instructions for enrolling and drafting; to file and preserve copies of all enrolment lists; to require stated reports of all proceedings on the part of his subordinates; to audit all accounts connected with the service under his direction; and to perform such other duties as the President may prescribe in carrying out the provisions of this act.

SEC. 7. And be it further enacted, That it shall be the duty of the provost-marshals to arrest all deserters, whether regulars, volunteers, militiamen, or persons called into the service under this or any other act of Congress, wherever they may be found, and to send them to the nearest military commander or military post; to detect, seize, and confine spies of the enemy, who shall without unreasonable delay be delivered to the custody of the general commanding the department in which they may be arrested, to be tried as soon as the exigencies of the service permit; to obey all lawful orders and regulations of the provost-marshal-general, and such as may be prescribed by law, concerning the enrolment and calling into service of the national forces.

SEC. 8. And be it further enacted, That in each of said districts there shall be a board of enrolment, to be composed of the provost-marshal, as president, and two other persons, to be appointed by the President of the United States, one of whom shall be a licensed and practising physician and surgeon.

SEC. 9. And be it further enacted, That it shall be the duty of the said board to pide the district into sub-districts of convenient size, if they shall deem it necessary, not exceeding two, without the direction of the Secretary of War, and to appoint, on or before the tenth day of March next, and in each alternate year thereafter, an enrolling officer for each sub-district, and to furnish him with proper blanks and instructions; and he shall immediately proceed to enroll all persons subject to military duty, noting their respective places of residence, ages on the first day of July following, and their occupation, and shall, on or before the first day of April, report the same to the board of enrolment, to be consolidated into one list, a copy of which shall be transmitted to the provost-marshal-general on or before the first day of May succeeding the enrolment: Provided, nevertheless, That if from any cause the duties prescribed by this section cannot be performed within the time specified, then the same shall be performed as soon thereafter as practicable.

SEC. 10. And be it further enacted, That the enrolment of each class shall be made separately and shall only embrace those whose ages shall be on the first day of July thereafter between twenty and forty-five years.

SEC. 11. And be it further enacted, That all persons thus enrolled shall be subject, for two years after the first day of July succeeding the enrolment, to be called into the military service of the United States, and to continue in service during the present rebellion, not, however, exceeding the term of three years; and when called into service shall be placed on the same footing, in all respects, as volunteers for three years, or during the war, including advance pay and bounty as now provided by law.

SEC. 12. And be it further enacted, That whenever it may be necessary to call out the national forces for military service, the President is hereby authorized to assign to each district the number of men to be furnished by said district; and thereupon the enrolling board shall, under the direction of the President, make a draft of the required number, and fifty per cent. in addition, and shall make an exact and complete roll of the names of the persons so drawn, and of the order in which they were drawn, so that the first drawn may stand first upon the said roll, and the second may stand second, and so on; and the persons so drawn shall be notified of the same within ten days thereafter, by a written or printed notice, to be served personally or by leaving a copy at the last place of residence, requiring them to appear at a designated rendezvous to report for duty. In assigning to the districts the number of men to be furnished therefrom, the President shall take into consideration the number of volunteers and militia furnished by and from the several states in which said districts are situated, and the period of their service since the commencement of the present rebellion, and shall so make said assignment as to equalize the numbers among the districts of the several states, considering and allowing for the numbers already furnished as aforesaid and the time of their service.

SEC. 13. And be it further enacted, That any person drafted and notified to appear as aforesaid, may, on or before the day fixed for his appearance, furnish an acceptable substitute to take his place in the draft; or he may pay to such person as the Secretary of War may authorize to receive it, such sum, not exceeding three hundred dollars, as the Secretary may determine, for the procuration of such substitute; which sum shall be fixed at a uniform rate by a general order made at the time of ordering a draft for any state or territory; and thereupon such person so furnishing the substitute, or paying the money, shall be discharged from further liability under that draft. And any person failing to report after due service of notice, as herein prescribed, without furnishing a substitute, or paying the required sum therefor, shall be deemed a deserter, and shall be arrested by the provost-marshal and sent to the nearest military post for trial by court-martial, unless, upon proper showing that he is not liable to do military duty, the board of enrolment shall relieve him from the draft.

SEC. 14. And be it further enacted, That all drafted persons shall, on arriving at the rendezvous, be carefully inspected by the surgeon of the board, who shall truly report to the board the physical condition of each one; and all persons drafted and claiming exemption from military duty on account of disability, or any other cause, shall present their claims to be exempted to the board, whose decision shall be final.

SEC. 15. And be it further enacted, That any surgeon charged with the duty of such inspection who shall receive from any person whomsoever any money or other valuable thing, or agree, directly or indirectly, to receive the same to his own or another's use for making an imperfect inspection or a false or incorrect report, or who shall willfully neglect to make a faithful inspection and true report, shall be tried by a court-martial, and, on conviction thereof, be punished by fine not exceeding five hundred dollars nor less than two hundred, and be imprisoned at the discretion of the court, and be cashiered and dismissed from the service.

SEC. 16. And be it further enacted, That as soon as the required number of able-bodied men liable to do military duty shall be obtained from the list of those drafted, the remainder shall be discharged; and all drafted persons reporting at the place of rendezvous shall be allowed travelling pay from their places of residence; and all persons discharged at the place of rendezvous shall be allowed travelling pay to their places of residence; and all expenses connected with the enrolment and draft, including subsistence while at the rendezvous, shall be paid from the appropriation for enrolling and drafting, under such regulations as the President of the United States shall prescribe; and all expenses connected with the arrest and return of deserters to their regiments, or such other duties as the provost-marshal shall be called upon to perform, shall be paid from the appropriation for arresting deserters, under such regulations as the President of the United States shall prescribe: Provided, The provost-marshals shall in no case receive commutation for transportation or for fuel and quarters, but only for forage, when not furnished by the government, together with actual expenses of postage, stationery, and clerk hire authorized by the provost-marshal-general.

SEC. 17. And be it further enacted, That any person enrolled and drafted according to the provisions of this act who shall furnish an acceptable substitute, shall thereupon receive from the board of enrolment a certificate of discharge from such draft, which shall exempt him from military duty during the time for which he was drafted; and such substitute shall be entitled to the same pay and allowances provided by law as if he had been originally drafted into the service of the United States.

SEC. 18. And be it further enacted, That such of the volunteers and militia now in the service of the United States as may reenlist to serve one year, unless sooner discharged, after the expiration of their present term of service, shall be entitled to a bounty of fifty dollars, one half of which to be paid upon such reenlistment, and the balance at the expiration of the term of reenlistment; and such as may reenlist to serve for two years, unless sooner discharged, after the expiration of their present term of enlistment, shall receive, upon such reenlistment, twenty-five dollars of the one hundred dollars bounty for enlistment provided by the fifth section of the act approved twenty-second of July, eighteen hundred and sixty-one, entitled "An act to authorize the employment of volunteers to aid in enforcing the laws and protecting public property."

SEC. 19. And be it further enacted, That whenever a regiment of volunteers of the same arm, from the same State, is reduced to one half the maximum number prescribed by law, the President may direct the consolidation of the companies of such regiment: Provided, That no company so formed shall exceed the Maximum number prescribed by law. When such consolidation is made, the regimental officers shall be reduced in proportion to the reduction in the number of companies.

SEC. 20. And be it further enacted, That whenever a regiment is reduced below the minimum number allowed by law, no officers shall be appointed in such regiment beyond those necessary for the command of such reduced number.

SEC. 21. And be it further enacted, That so much of the fifth section of the act approved seventeenth July, eighteen hundred and sixty-two, entitled, "An act to amend an act calling forth the militia to execute the laws of the Union," and so forth, as requires the approval of the President to carry into execution the sentence of a court-martial, be, and the same is hereby, repealed, as far as relates to carrying into execution the sentence of any court-martial against any person convicted as a spy or deserter, or of mutiny or murder; and hereafter sentences in punishment of these offences may be carried into execution upon the approval of the commanding general in the field.

SEC. 22. And be it further enacted, That courts-martial shall have power to sentence officers who shall absent themselves from their commands without leave, to be reduced to the ranks to serve three years or during the war.

SEC. 23. And be it further enacted, That the clothes, arms, military outfits, and accoutrements furnished by the United States to any soldier, shall not be sold, bartered, exchanged, pledged, loaned, or given away; and no person not a soldier, or duly authorized officer of the United States, who has possession of any such clothes, arms, military outfits, or accoutrements, furnished as aforesaid, and which have been the subjects of any such sale, barter, exchange, pledge, loan, or gift, shall have any right, title, or interest therein; but the same may be seized and taken wherever found by any officer of the United States, civil or military, and shall thereupon be delivered to any quartermaster, or other officer authorized to receive the same; and the possession of any such clothes, arms, military outfits, or accoutrements, by any person not a soldier or officer of the United States, shall be prima facie evidence of such a sale, barter, ex-, change, pledge, loan, or gift, as aforesaid.

SEC. 24. And be it further enacted, That every person not subject to the rules and articles of war who shall procure or entice, or attempt to procure or entice, a soldier in the service of the United States to desert; or who shall harbor, conceal, or give employment to a deserter, or carry him away, or aid in carrying him away, knowing him to be such; or who shall purchase from any soldier his arms, equipments, ammunition, uniform, clothing, or any part thereof; and any captain or commanding officer of any ship or vessel, or any superintendent or conductor of any railroad, or any other public conveyance, carrying away any such soldier as one of his crew or otherwise, knowing him to have deserted, or shall refuse to deliver him up to the orders of his commanding officer, shall, upon legal conviction, be fined, at the discretion of any court having cognizance of the same, in any sum not exceeding five hundred dollars, and he shall be imprisoned not exceeding two years nor less than six months.

SEC. 25. And be it further enacted, That if any person shall resist any draft of men enrolled under this act into the service of the United States, or shall counsel or aid any person to resist any such draft; or shall assault or obstruct any officer in making such draft, or in the performance of any service in relation thereto; or shall counsel any person to assault or obstruct any such officer, or shall counsel any drafted men not to appear at the place of rendezvous, or willfully dissuade them from the performance of military duty as required by law, such person shall be subject to summary arrest by the provost-marshal, and shall be forthwith delivered to the civil authorities, and, upon conviction thereof, be punished by a fine not exceeding five hundred dollars, or by imprisonment not exceeding two years, or by both of said punishments.

SEC. 26. And be it further enacted, That, immediately after the passage of this act, the President shall issue his proclamation declaring that all soldiers now absent from their regiments without leave may return within a time specified to such place or places as he may indicate in his proclamation, and be restored to their respective regiments without punishment, except the forfeiture of their pay and allowances during their absence; and all deserters who shall not return within the time so specified by the President shall, upon being arrested, be punished as the law provides.

SEC. 27. And be it further enacted, That depositions of witnesses residing beyond the limits of the state, territory, or district in which military courts shall be ordered to sit, may be taken in cases not capital by either party, and read in evidence; provided the same shall be taken upon reasonable notice to the opposite party, and duly authenticated.

SEC. 28. And be it further enacted, That the judge advocate shall have power to appoint a reporter, whose duty it shall be to record the proceedings of, and testimony taken before military courts instead of the judge advocate; and such reporter may take down such proceedings and testimony in the first instance in shorthand. The reporter shall be sworn or affirmed faithfully to perform his duty before entering upon it.

SEC. 29. And be it further enacted, That the court shall, for reasonable cause, grant a continuance to either party for such time and as often as shall appear to be just: Provided, That if the prisoner be in close confinement, the trial shall not be delayed for a period longer than sixty days.

SEC. 30. And be it further enacted, That in time of war, insurrection, or rebellion, murder, assault and battery with an intent to kill, manslaughter, mayhem, wounding by shooting or stabbing with an intent to commit murder, robbery, arson, burglary, rape, assault and battery with an intent to commit rape, and larceny, shall be punishable by the sentence of a general court-martial or military commission, when committed by persons who are in the military service of the United States, and subject to the articles of war; and the punishments for such offences shall never be less than those inflicted by the laws of the state, territory, or district in which they may have been committed.

SEC. 31. And be it further enacted, That any officer absent from duty with leave, except for sickness or wounds, shall, during his absence, receive half of the pay and allowances prescribed by law, and no more; and any officer absent without leave shall, in addition to the penalties prescribed by law or a court-martial, forfeit all pay or allowances during such absence.

SEC. 32. And be it further enacted, That the commanders of regiments and of batteries in the field, are hereby authorized and empowered to grant furloughs for a period not exceeding thirty days at any one time to five per centum of the non-commissioned officers and privates, for good conduct in the line of duty, and subject to the approval of the commander of the forces of which such non-commissioned officers and privates form a part.

SEC. 33. And be it further enacted, That the President of the United States is hereby authorized and empowered, during the present rebellion, to call forth the national forces, by draft, in the manner provided for in this act.

SEC. 34. And be it further enacted, That all persons drafted under the provisions of this act shall be assigned by the President to military duty in such corps, regiments, or other branches of the service as the exigencies of the service may require.

SEC. 35. And be it further enacted, That hereafter details to special service shall only be made with the consent of the commanding officer of forces in the field; and enlisted men, now or hereafter detailed to special service, shall not receive any extra pay for such services beyond that allowed to other enlisted men.

SEC. 36. And be it further enacted, That general orders of the War Department, numbered one hundred and fifty-four and one hundred and sixty-two, in reference to enlistments from the volunteers into the regular service, be, and the same are hereby, rescinded; and hereafter no such enlistments shall be allowed.

SEC. 37. And be it further enacted, That the grades created in the cavalry forces of the United States by section eleven of the act approved seventeenth July, eighteen hundred and sixty-two, and for which no rate of compensation has been provided, shall be paid as follows, to wit: Regimental commissary the same as regimental quartermaster; chief trumpeter the same as chief bugler; sad[d]ler-sergeant the same as regimental commissary-sergeant; company commissary-sergeant the same as company quartermaster's-sergeant: Provided, That the grade of supernumerary second lieutenant, and two teamsters for each company, and one chief farrier and blacksmith for each regiment, as allowed by said section of that act, be, and they are hereby, abolished ; and each cavalry company may have two trumpeters, to be paid as buglers; and each regiment shall have one veterinary surgeon, with the rank of a regimental sergeant-major, whose compensation shall be seventy-five dollars per month.

SEC. 38. And be it further enacted, That all persons who, in time of war or of rebellion against the supreme authority of the United States, shall be found lurking or acting as spies, in or about any of the fortifications, posts, quarters, or encampments of any of the armies of the United States, or elsewhere, shall be triable by a general court-martial or military commission, and shall, upon conviction, suffer death.

APPROVED, March 3, 1863